"Got to cut through the jungle and sneak up on 'im," said Sam. He and I flung the two ropes over our shoulders. Then Sam motioned us to follow him.

"Wait," Louise said. "Somebody has to call the sheriff."

That made sense, and I knew who could handle that job. "So take my bike and do it," I said.

"We'll use our phone at Deepwood House," Jeep said in a hurry.

The girls took off faster than you could sneeze. I figured they didn't mind missing the walk through the jungle. I didn't much care to push through briars and snaky bogs, either.

Sam and I stayed close to the lane, though. As long as we had to watch for snakes and such, there wasn't time to think of what might happen later. It was when we stopped that I got trembling scared.

There are three things that remain—faith, hope,
and love—and the greatest of these is love.
I Corinthians 13:13 (TLB)

A MIRROR MOUNTAIN ADVENTURE

# MYSTERY
## AT DEEPWOOD BAY

### WYNNETTE FRASER

Chariot Books™
David C. Cook Publishing Co.

Chariot Books™ is an imprint of David C. Cook Publishing Co.
David C. Cook Publishing Co., Elgin, Illinois 60120
David C. Cook Publishing Co., Weston, Ontario
Nova Distribution Ltd., Torquay, England

MYSTERY AT DEEPWOOD BAY
© 1992 by Wynnette Fraser.

Designed by Elizabeth Thompson
Cover illustration by Wendy Wassink Ackison

First Printing, 1992
Printed in the United States of America
96 95 94 93 92  5 4 3 2 1

**Library of Congress Cataloging-in-Publication Data**
Fraser, Wynnette, 1925-
    Mystery at Deepwood Bay / Wynnette Fraser.
        p.   cm.—(A Mirror Mountain adventure)
    Summary: When Johnny and Louise leave Mirror Mountain to look
after their depressed uncle Jake on an island off the coast of South
Carolina, they begin an investigation into church vandalism.
    ISBN 1-55513-717-2
    1. Mystery and detective stories.[1. Sea Islands—Fiction. 2. Christian
life—Fiction.]I. Title. II. Series.
PZ7.F8647Mx 1992
[Fic]—dc20                                              91-30621
                                                           CIP
                                                            AC

# Contents

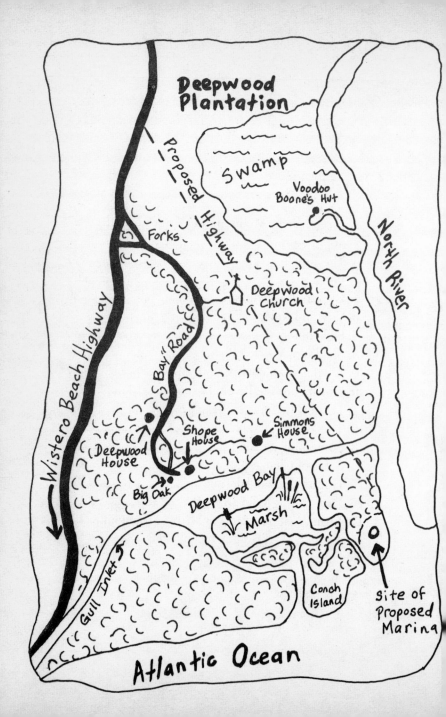

# 1
# From Mirror Mountain to Wistero Island

My twelfth birthday was a mite upsetting. Aunt Lou always said bad things come in threes. Maybe surprises come in twos. I don't know. What I do know is that two of them at one time can be downright worrisome, especially when you have to give up one and can't keep the surprise you fancy most.

I got my first birthday surprise at our church on the mountain. It used to be Uncle Elbert's cabin. Sandy McRee, our preacher, stayed there all winter and drove Louise and me to school every day. Now Sandy was living in the dorm at Cougarville College. Two forestry students from Jimson University were moving into the back rooms of the church.

Hank and Rusty had stayed there last summer, too.

Now they were back again, trying to save the trees that were dying on the top of Mirror Mountain. Since I plan to be a conservationist myself someday, I asked Rusty if I could help them. I told him I wanted to work just for the learning, but he said they had money donated to pay a helper, and it might as well be me.

It was like God had dropped a miracle on my head. The Lord sure knows the Finlays don't have to look for places to use money.

I was so excited, I ran all the way home. Midnight, Aunt Lou's clumsy old black dog, bumped alongside me. He pretty near knocked me down more than once, but I didn't care.

School had been out for two weeks. My school friends Scott and Willis would be at Camp Walking Tall for most of the summer. Things were pretty much back to normal at our little grey house on Mirror Mountain. After flying off the mountain on a hang glider, Pa had given Ma his word that he wouldn't take any more fool chances for a while. He was working overtime at Uncle Elbert's Highway Store and bringing home more money than ever before. It was plain to all of us that Pa was doing everything he could to make life better for us.

The sky was full of blue and purple and pink as the sun was getting ready to set. I was glad to see Old Blue, Pa's station wagon, in the yard. That meant Pa was home to hear my good news along with Ma and Louise.

"Guess what!" I yelled. Midnight barked as I jumped from the bottom to the top steps of the back porch where they were. "I got a job! Hank and Rusty are gonna pay me to help save the trees. Ain't that something?"

I stood there panting worse than Midnight. Sweat ran down my face as I waited for somebody to say hooray. Nobody did. That was when it hit me; the mood on that porch wasn't right for horn tooting just then.

Ma put down the corn shock mat she was weaving. Louise set down her guitar. I saw what looked like a letter in my sister's hand, and Ma had the envelope. From the looks on their faces, I figured the news in that letter had to be heavy.

"D-did somebody die?" I asked.

"No, Johnny Elbert," said Ma. "But my Uncle Jake needs our help."

Then I got my second surprise. It was already decided. Louise and I were going on the bus to Wistero Island soon as we could get packed, maybe tomorrow. The way Ma said it, you'd have thought we did that kind of thing all the time. Why, I had hardly spent more than a night or two off the mountain in my whole life. Ma said we might need to stay a month or two! And not once had I been asked what I thought about it.

Now that I knew nobody was actually dead, I figured I had a right to be a bit contrary. "Send Louise now," I said. "I'll go when my job's over in July." When Ma shook her head, my voice got louder. "Didn't anybody hear what I just said? I got myself a paying job, people!"

Ma said she heard, but no, we couldn't wait. That letter Louise had just read was from Sae Simmons, a neighbor of Uncle Jake's. Mrs. Simmons was a nurse. She said Uncle Jake had gotten over his heart attack, but he was depressed. He was forgetting to take his medicine and needed somebody to see he ate right.

Ma said she couldn't leave home now because she had Aunt Lou to look after. "It's just a blessing you and Louise are responsible enough to take on this job, Johnny Elbert. If you wasn't, I don't know what we'd do."

Pa nodded his head. "You younguns been pestering me to take you to the ocean long as I can recollect," he said. "Well, here's your chance."

Wistero Island is five hours away from Mirror Mountain. We never had enough money to go that far just to be going. Ma went down on the bus to be with Uncle Jake when Aunt Mollie died. She ended up staying longer than she started out to because their boy, Lester, was killed in a plane crash coming home for his ma's funeral.

My heart felt like a balloon somebody squeezed the air out of. It wasn't that I thought my job was more important than Uncle Jake needing help. The thing was, I couldn't see that tough old uncle of Ma's needing anybody to take care of him. Not ever.

Last time he was on the mountain, he walked all over it. He never seemed to get tired. I'm talking about a man who took care of a big island plantation for years and years. After he retired, he ran shell tours with his boat. Four or five times a day, people paid him to take them to a little island. "Just for the fun of hunting shells," he told me.

Uncle Jake was tall like Ma, with grey eyes and brown hair that had started turning grey. Every time he and Aunt Mollie and Lester came to see us, he asked us to visit them on the island. I kept hoping Pa would find a way to take him up on it. That was before Lester joined the Navy and Aunt Mollie got sick. After that, Uncle Jake had not come back to the mountain anymore. He lived by himself at Deepwood Bay. Ma still wrote to him, but he never wrote her back.

"It must be awful to lose all your family," Louise said as she brushed back that long, yellow hair she loves to shake around. "No wonder he had a heart attack. I'm just glad I can cook and keep house. Maybe I can help him that way."

I hate it when Louise makes me look bad. "What makes you think I don't want to help Uncle Jake, Miss Perfect? It ain't like you got to give up anything important to go. That old guitar you love so much can go right along with you to Deepwood Bay."

I felt Pa's hand on my shoulder. "Hold on there,

11

son. Old Jake always seemed to think right much of you. If anybody can get him to start up them shell tours again, it's more than likely to be you. He's your Ma's only living uncle, and . . ."

I knew what was coming next, so I beat him to it. "I know, Pa. 'Family's family and no Finlay nor Shope ever lets down blood kin.' I'll go tell Hank and Rusty I can't help 'em this summer." Saying it didn't come easy.

Ma came over and stooped to hug my neck. She and Louise tend to be tall. She had to stoop because I'm short and chunky like Pa. "That's my Johnny talking now," she said. "I knew I could count on you to do what's right. And I'm sorry as I can be you got to give up your job. I know how much it means to you."

All of a sudden, Midnight jumped up from the steps and took off across the yard. When we heard his hello bark, Ma's hands flew to her cheeks. "Oh, Earle!" she almost hollered at Pa. "I plumb forgot to send you to the cabin to fetch your Aunt Lou, and here she comes totin' a cake. She don't have a bit of business walking up here when she don't have to."

Pa hurried to help Aunt Lou, and Ma turned to me. "Johnny, you can wait till morning to give up that job. A boy don't turn twelve but once in his life, and we're gonna celebrate."

There was no way I could stay grumpy when everybody was heaping good wishes on me. Aunt Lou never would hear of anyone else making or decorating one of our birthday cakes. To go with the cake, Ma brought out a churn of homemade ice cream. I liked my presents, too, even if they were just clothes.

To wrap up the evening Finlay style, Pa and Louise played their guitars. We sang hymns and folk songs till the sun went down and the air got dark and too cool for Aunt Lou.

"It's prayer time, Earle," she told Pa. "After that, you can drive me home."

We held hands while Pa prayed, "Lord, we praise You. You been good to this family. We know You want to use our younguns to bless Uncle Jake, Lord. It appears he needs a lot of Your love to heal him." Pa's voice choked. "It ain't easy for us, Lord, sending Louise and Johnny somewhere that's strange to them. You know better'n anybody how much we gonna miss 'em. That's why we countin' on You to keep them out of harm's way. And please get 'em back home soon's You see fit. We pray in the blessed name of Jesus." Everybody said amen.

What Pa said about missing us went to bed with me that night. I had thought twelve was most grown, but I'm older now and I know I was just a scared little youngun. It all just happened too fast. I knew I would miss Ma and Pa and Aunt Lou. I would miss old Midnight scratching on my window in the morning. The people that loved me most were on Mirror Mountain, and I didn't know what we could expect to find on an island called Wistero.

# 2
# Super Sam

It was funny that Pa mentioned I might get Uncle Jake back to running shell tours. I never could tear myself away from watching boats on TV. When I didn't have anything else to do, I would go sit on the big log over Way High Creek and play like I was running a boat across a big lake.

Sitting next to Louise on the bus going down, the idea of me running Uncle Jake's boat kept growing bigger and bigger inside my head. "Johnny Elbert Finlay," I could hear him say, "you are something else again." I couldn't imagine him being anything but proud of me. We always had such good times together when he and Aunt Mollie and their boy, Lester, visited us on the mountain. But like Sandy McRee used to read from the Bible, I reckon there's a time for all kind of things to begin and end.

Uncle Jake didn't meet us at the Wistero Beach Bus Station. Instead he sent Sam, the son of Sae Simmons who had written to Ma. We followed Sam to Gull Inlet Landing. Uncle Jake was waiting in the boat and didn't look as glad to see us as I had counted on. It was like he saw me every day and hardly knew I was there.

I tried to tell myself Ma's uncle just didn't feel good, so I grinned as I put out one foot to step into the boat. The boat moved, and I sat squash down in the mud. If Uncle Jake hadn't noticed me before, he and everyone else sure noticed that dumb stunt.

After we had been on the island for a week, I wondered if Uncle Jake had left and some stranger was using his body. He just wasn't the same frisky old guy I remembered. Nothing I said or did got him excited about fishing or anything else. His crusty hair was almost white. He hardly ever combed it, and sometimes it looked like frostbit grass. He sat around all day in pajamas so baggy the pants couldn't hold onto his skinny hips. Uncle Jake hardly ever smiled. My dictionary says depressed means "sad and gloomy," and that fit Ma's uncle to a tee. Just being 'round him was starting to make me feel the same way.

Louise didn't have a bit of trouble taking over Uncle Jake's house and running it like she wanted to. Before we left home, Ma made me promise to help my sister all I could, but soon as we got the kitchen cleaned up every morning, Louise couldn't wait to get me out of the way. She was fourteen but bossy to beat twenty.

Sam Simmons was my first new friend at Deepwood Bay. We had been there about a week when he asked me to walk with him to check his papa's church way back in the plantation woods. The church was being hit by vandals about every weekend, he said. So far, nobody had any idea who the vandals were. About all Sam could do was check for what damage had been done and report it to his papa, Preacher Abe, so it could be cleaned up or fixed before the next service.

I wasn't sure about leaving Uncle Jake to go with Sam. But Louise said Ma and Pa would be proud of me for helping Sam keep watch on a church. "I can handle things here," she told me.

At the supper table, I asked Uncle Jake if he minded my going, and he said it was okay with him. "Give you something to do besides pestering me to act your age," he said, waving his bony fingers at me. "Preacher Abe's a good man of God," he went on. "Did I ever tell you how the plantation slaves came to build Deepwood Church?"

I started to say he told us when he was on the mountain, but Louise was back of him warning me I'd better not. He looked more perky tonight after he had taken a bath and put on clean pajamas.

I was mixing ketchup into my second helping of grits. Uncle Jake wasn't hungry enough for seconds. Louise sat down so he'd know we were both listening to him.

"Old Henry Duncan owned this plantation," he said, "and Preacher Abe Simmons's great, great grandfather, Joshua Simmons, was one of his wife's yard slaves. Her name was Lucretia." He stopped and stared into space a full minute, then blinked and went on. "Joshua Simmons was the gardener. Mrs. Lucretia taught him to read and write. Well, they say old Henry didn't like that worth a hoot. He wasn't for educating slaves." Uncle Jake took a deep breath and blew it out slow-like. "It wasn't long till that there Joshua got to reading his Bible and praying. Then he told Lucretia he wanted to build a church for his own people."

Uncle Jake heaved his wide, bony shoulders and let out a mournful sigh. "Up till then, all the slaves sat in the balcony at white people's churches. Lucretia asked Henry to help Jacob get his church built and . . ."

This was taking too long. "What did old Henry say?" I asked.

"He said no." Uncle Jake coughed. "But Lucretia figured another way. Joshua painted first-rate pictures, and the Gullah women wove sweet grass baskets to sell. They'd learned to do that in Africa. Lucretia sold 'em to the summer folks."

"Uncle Jake," Louise said, "Sam told us he was of Gullah descent. Who are the Gullah?"

"The Gullah were slaves brought over from Sierra Leone on the African Rice Coast. Plantation owners on the islands of Georgia and South Carolina bought 'em off the ships. We think the name Gullah was from a tribe called Gola. They mixed their way of talkin' with what English their owners taught 'em."

We waited to hear more, but a sad look came into Uncle Jake's eyes like he was thinking of something that didn't have anything to do with what he'd just told us. "I'm about done for," he said, pushing his chair back. With one hand, he held on to the waist of his loose pajama pants. "I'll see you younguns tomorrow."

He didn't look too steady, so Louise reached out to help him. But he moved away from her, and it looked like he did it on purpose.

After he crossed the hall and shut himself in his room, Louise said, "I guess I'll have to take up all them pajama pants of his 'fore he falls trying to hold 'em up." That wasn't supposed to be funny, but we laughed anyhow.

The next morning, I was up early and dressed for hiking.

Uncle Jake's one-story house had big rooms full of old furniture. A hall split the front part from the back. The only bathroom was on the back side between two bedrooms, Uncle Jake's and Lester's, which stayed locked.

A screen porch ran all the way across the front, looking out on the bay. Back of the porch on one end was the big kitchen. It had old-fashioned cabinets and a big wooden table. But the sink was new, and there was an electric stove and refrigerator. Louise loved the washing machine, but it made an awful racket and near about walked across the room when it was on spin.

Louise slept in the dining room where nobody ate, and I put my cot on the porch outside the window of the old sitting room where nobody sat.

It was my job to wake Uncle Jake and see that he took his medicine every morning. His room was across from the kitchen. It had a tall wooden wardrobe and two chests of drawers, one high and one low. The low one had a mirror that swung up and down.

His heavy iron bed was on a sleeping porch that jutted off the room like the barrel of a shotgun. On shelves under the windows by his bed was more junk than I could name: flashlight, jars of fishhooks, lures, corks, shoes and shoe polish kit, rubbing alcohol, cough syrup, fishing magazines. That kind of stuff. There was a Bible, but it was dusty like everything else. Louise said nobody could find nothing in all that clutter. She kept his medicine in the kitchen.

That morning when I came back from Uncle Jake's room, my sister was scrubbing the sink and humming. I looked past her through the window. I could see Uncle Jake's boat still tied up by the boat house at the landing.

She turned her head to one side. "Did he take his medicine all right?"

"Same's always. Hooped 'em in, washed 'em down,

and went back to sleep." I picked up the broom to sweep the kitchen.

Louise's yellow ponytail moved every time her head did. "It's not good, Johnny. When he's not sleeping or eating, he just sits and stares at the bay. . . ."

"Or the TV set," I finished. "But he was winding up last night for a while." I didn't mention how weak his voice had gotten, or how he stopped in the middle of saying things. It had come to me that Uncle Jake might not get well. I didn't want to think about that.

"We've got to find a way to get him out of this house," Louise said. I looked up from pushing the broom and saw her squinting out the window with her hands over her eyes. In a piece of a minute, she started giggling.

"What's so funny?"

"Sam. I get so tickled when I see his big old T-shirt coming this way!"

I grinned. "I reckon he's somewhere under it." I swept sand and crumbs into the dustpan like crazy.

"John-Eeeh." That was how Sam hollered my name. Nobody had ever called me John E. before.

I slapped the dustpan and broom on their hooks and made for the door.

Sam was the great, great, great grandson of old Joshua Simmons, or as he put it, "triply great grandson." He wasn't like any friend I had back at Cougarville Elementary. He had reddish-brown skin like Sae, who was part Wistero Indian.

Like his triply great grandfather, Sam could draw anything he saw. The face he had painted on the big T-shirt was his own. He got it right, too, except for the mouth. It was stretched wide open, baring sharp wildcat teeth. He had set that off by neatly printing SUPER SAM under it. Grayish splotches were all over his yellow baseball cap. So there would be no mistaking what those splotches stood for, TOUGH GULLS was printed above the bill in big letters. Even his sneakers sported bright fish and seashells. Next to him, my faded shirt and jeans must have looked mighty flat. His dark hair wasn't real long or curly. He had string-beany arms and legs. Though Sam was just eleven, he was already taller than me. The top of my head barely came up to his high cheekbones.

I opened the door.

"How you do," said Sam with a wide grin. "It appeahs Mister Jake's not taking 'is boat out today."

Sam's "boat out" sounded like "boot ote." Uncle Jake said it was Gullah talk, left over from Sam's slave ancestors. He never pronounced the "h" before he, his, or him. It rattled me some, but I didn't have any room to say so. Back home our schoolmates made fun of our mountain talk, but we did say our r's. Sam called our state "Soth Cah'lina." But I reckon most of his grammar was better than mine. Sae and Preacher Abe saw to it. They'd been to college.

Sam did love to get me riled up, especially concerning Uncle Jake's boat.

"You know Uncle Jake don't think I got enough sense to handle his old motorboat," I snapped.

He just kept on grinning. "Don't hit me, John E., but you do remember you did not show much promise for boating the day you came? You do recall how you missed the boat and went swoosh into Gull Inlet?" Sam's eyes glowed like a cat's might when it stalks a sparrow.

I felt like socking him one, but I couldn't do that to the best friend I had found on the island. In the past week, we had gone crabbing in the marshes. He picked me up every day to ride with him in the Simmonses' *Chariot*. That was the name painted on their boat. We would take Preacher Abe to his weekday job at Wistero Beach Post Office. Coming back, Sam gave me boating lessons.

"You learn fast," he told me. "Soon you'll be ready to handle Mr. Jake's boat by yourself." I could tell he wasn't teasing. He meant it.

"What I really want," I told Sam, "is to show Uncle Jake I can take shell hunters to Conch Island. Even if he don't feel like going along. So far, he acts like he ain't never gonna run tours no more."

Sam put his hands together. His long middle fingers tapped each other in slow motion. "That's hard to say, John E. I miss ole Jake's jokin' and laughin' like 'e used to, myself. 'E always loved this island and all its history. Maybe Jake'll soon snap to being 'is old self again. Anyway, Sae and Papa say so." Sam yanked his cap off, then slapped it back on. "Let's go, man. If we

22

hurry, we'll get past Deepwood House 'fore that pesky Yankee girl sees us. Bye-bye, Looo-weese." He waved past my shoulder at my nosy sister who was eavesdropping as usual.

Louise snorted. "You boys might be glad for a sharp Yankee gal like Jeep Clark to protect you in that jungle." Now, a remark like that was uncalled for and downright insulting. I wasn't about to let her get away with it.

My sister has long legs. I bided my time till we got far enough to outrun her. Then I turned, did a silly dance and rapped:

"Chicken-hen, chicken-hen standin' in the breeze.

"Chicken-hen a'cacklin' and her name be LOOO-WEESE!"

Sam chimed in on the last word, which was how he said my sister's name. I didn't have to tell him it was time to run.

# 3
# The Jungle

We didn't need girls on our hike, much less a bossy one from Connecticut. I had already met Jeep Clark, and she ran her mouth equal to Louise, only faster.

Uncle Jake had told me Deepwood was one of the oldest plantations on the island. It was kept up by selling off beef cattle. Uncle Jake said he hoped he never had to see it ripped up for development like most of the others.

According to Sam, this was the second summer Jeep and her dad stayed in an apartment at Deepwood House. That was the big old home built by the first slaves on the plantation. It sat off Bay Road, an unpaved road that wiggled for miles through the jungle from Deepwood Bay to the beach highway.

Tom Clark was a science professor at a college called Fairmont. I hadn't seen him yet. Jeep said her dad didn't get out much. She told us he was too busy writing a book for Meg Duncan, who owned Deepwood Plantation. Meg owned a big publishing company in New York, too. She lived in New York and only visited Deepwood House once in a while. Sam told me she had hired a Charleston lawyer to be in charge of the plantation affairs.

"Sherman Attaway comes zooming in off and on in one of them little foreign sports cars," he said.

We reached the big oak where Uncle Jake's clearing met Bay Road. The Simmonses' driveway was on our right. Sam said we were going to take a shortcut through the jungle. "No use going by Deepwood House," he said.

I followed him down his driveway a little ways, then he turned left on a weedy path. I went after him but wished we were on Mirror Mountain. Up there he would have had to follow me.

The woods was rightly called the jungle. Wisteria vines big as my arm crawled over everything. They looked tough enough for Tarzan to swing on. Rabbits and squirrels kept running away from us.

"Air's getting heavy," Sam said. "We must be near the old cemetery. Now don't get scared, John E."

"Scared of what?" I asked, but I knew what he was talking about. Uncle Jake had told me how old-time Gullah people buried their dead in the deep woods. They had all kinds of stories about ghosts. He said it was because of beliefs they brought over from Africa.

"Sam," I said, "mountain people got plenty of ghost stories, too. We thought a hermit's ghost was haunting Mirror Mountain. Turns out it was a bum stealing Aunt Lou's chickens. She caught him and made him work for his rations."

Sam snickered along with me. "I used to be scared

I'd step on a grave hid under the vines and have some
bad spirit jump up an' attack me. But Papa says it ain't
so. 'E says Christians better don't fool 'round with
voodoo magic. 'E read it from the Bible how God
forbids it. I s'pose Voodoo Boone's the only witch
doctor left 'round these parts."

"Oh, yeah. I heard about her from Uncle Jake." All
the mountain people had loved Uncle Jake's island
ghost stories. "You mean to say she's still living?"

"Last I heard, Maum Beulah was still stirring up
magic potions wa-a-ay back near the North River. She
won't listen to Papa's preaching."

Sam's shortcut was taking too long. I was right glad
when we pulled back onto Bay Road, but I knew he
had goofed when we came out right in front of
Deepwood House. To keep Jeep from seeing us, we
ducked behind some bushes along the road.

The big house looked like a gingerbread castle. It
was tall, with a little railed porch at the top. Sam called
it a widow's walk.

A brassy-haired woman sat on the wide front porch.
She moved her hands like she was sewing something.
In the yard, a big man buzzed a weed-eater 'round
the flower beds. His fat head was bald down the
middle. What hair he did have on the sides and back
was long and stringy.

"That's Slag and Irene Hatton," Sam said.
"Sherman hired 'em for caretakers last fall. They stay
in the downstairs apartment on the right."

I looked at the windows of the left upstairs apartment where Sam said Jeep lived. I didn't see anything move.

We hurried down the road. The air that steamed out of the jungle had a mixed-up smell of hot pine needles and fishy bogs. I stopped to pick a blackberry runner from my sneaker string, then tightened it.

Sam waited for me, puffing. "'Eh, man, stop diddling along. The church lane's just 'round the next curve."

It was Friday. Sam said the vandals hadn't struck for more than a week. Deepwood Bible Church was so far back in the jungle, I didn't see how vandals found it in the first place.

"Sam, it don't make sense to me. Who'd come way back in these woods to trash up a little old church? You said you thought it was teenagers?"

"Papa says it's not right to point fingers at anybody. 'E says you got to have proof first. Vick and Kevin are jerky dudes. They live on Gull Inlet in ritzy houses and got speedboats. They race 'em and scare people most to death. Then they laugh like crazy. I'd say they might think it was real cool to dirty up black people's churches for kicks!"

"If I thought I'd get a charge trashing up any building," I said, "I sure enough wouldn't pick a church."

"Me, neither. I don't guess Vick or Kevin's scared of the devil 'imself, much less the Lord."

When we got to the church turnoff, we ran into Jeep, or you might say she almost ran into us. She was on her bike, and we were lucky it had good brakes.

27

"They tore up the sign!" She yelled. "It's on the ground." Her blue eyes were wide and excited.

I hadn't noticed till then what a little spit of a girl she was to be thirteen. Her curly hair was cut short like a boy's. It was brown, but pretty much the color of ground red pepper. Her big T-shirt was so long you couldn't tell what color shorts she wore. All the skin you could see on her was tanned and smooth, except for her turned-up nose. It was spattered with freckles, and sweat drops stood on each and every one of them. I didn't realize I was staring till our eyes met. Then my face got hot. I looked down at the handlebars of her ten-speed and pushed back the string of hay-brown hair that never stayed off my forehead.

"N-nice bike," I stammered, hoping Sam wouldn't see my red face.

He didn't. My friend was already walking fast down the lane toward the church.

"Jeep Clark," he hollered, "you just couldn't wait to tell us that bad news, could you? Well, me and John E.'s here to make our own investigation!"

Sam kept right on going, not waiting for her to answer.

# 4
# Vandals

As I ran to catch up with Sam, Jeep whizzed past us on her bike. Big oak trees hooked elbows over the long church lane. It was like walking the hallway of a haunted castle. No wonder island people let their minds chew on spooky stuff. The gray moss looked like beards on ghosts.

"We just wasted time trying to dodge Jeep," I told Sam.

"Appeahs so." Sam's long neck didn't budge when he nodded. "Like Papa says, 'Yankees talk fast, argue fast, and move fast.'"

"Kinda makes my head twirl."

"I know. Sae says fast talk's apt to hurt people's feelings sometimes when no hurt's intended. She says to treat words like sacks of fresh-picked beans. Don't spread 'em around till they been weighed."

When we got to the churchyard, Jeep was waiting by the torn-down sign. The post was split in two and mud was smeared over the words DEEPWOOD BIBLE CHURCH.

"No, no, no-hh!" hollered Sam. He stood over the sign with his hands on his hips. "I painted that sign!"

Jeep took a deep breath. "We can clean up the sign okay, but that post has had it."

She was right about that. I looked around, then pointed to the fat trunk of a pine tree. "How 'bout nailing it to that?" I asked Sam.

He halfway nodded, clenching his teeth. Every second, his face got more mean, like the one on his shirt. "Rich white brats!" he said under his breath.

Jeep reached into the pocket of her shorts for a Kleenex. I breathed easier to see she really did have on shorts under that floppy shirt. "Sam, you don't have one clue as to who did this," she told him. "I know you think it's Vick and Kevin, but it could just as well be someone you'd least suspect. Maybe someone black."

"Well, excuse me, Genevieve," he drawled, tipping his cap at her. His face had mischief written all over it. Sam could turn from being mad to being funny real fast.

Jeep's mouth went tight like she was trying not to laugh at his put-on grin. "Samuel Hezekiah Simmons,

30

if I weren't down on my knees trying to clean your church's sign, I'd cram this mud in your mouth for calling me that. Why don't you guys go check the church and stop pestering me?"

"Sam's gonna stop being a pest," I told her, not looking at him.

Over in one corner of the yard was a pipe with water flowing from it into a long concrete trough. Near the top of the trough, the water drained through a hole and down a little gully into the woods. A bucket hung on a post beside the pipe.

"I'll fetch some water from the flowing well," I told Jeep. "Then we'll wash down the sign for you."

"Gee, Johnny, that's nice of you." She smiled and I could feel my face heating up again. Maybe it was just because the air was so hot. I ran over to the well and dipped the bucket in the trough. Sam came after me and laid his hand back of the water coming from the pipe. He brayed like a donkey when it splashed over me. I sloshed some water from the pail at him and brayed right back. That went on till we were both wet. Nobody cared. The hot air would dry us off fast.

"Hey, you guys, do I have to come for that water myself?" I heard Jeep call.

"Coming right now." I took the pail of water over and swished it on the sign. Then we balled up pine straw and rubbed it over the sign to loosen the rest of the mud. The sign looked good as new, so we stood it against a pine till we could find nails and a hammer.

The little wooden church sat high off the ground on funny-looking stones. Sam said they were tabby blocks, made from sand and seashells. "My triply great grandpapa and other slaves laid the blocks first. Then they put the church together with wooden pegs."

Up on the mountain, I had come to like the kind of history that was passed down by word of mouth. Right then, I let my mind go way back in time. I pictured the Gullah people mixing sand and shells to build the big tabby blocks. I could almost hear them singing as they laid the foundation.

As we started toward the church, I noticed something. "Sam, was that shutter hanging like that before?" I pointed to an open window by the steps. The shutter hung by its top hinge like somebody had yanked it away to crawl through the window from the steps. When we got there, we found a jagged hole in the glass just above the latch. The window was still open.

"The dirty rats got inside!" Jeep yelled.

Sam fished through both pockets of his short jeans. "Oh, shucks, I must've forgot the key." His face had a sick look on it.

I strutted forward. "Have no fear—Johnny's here!" I bragged.

I flung myself over the rail by the top step and through the open window. I hit the floor inside with a thud, just missing a piece of broken glass. In the skimpy light, I tried the door. Had I not been so bent on showing off, I might have thought to do that in the first place. It was unlocked.

What we found inside was dirt, sticks, stones, and dirty rags all over the oak floor and furniture. Toilet paper that looked used was strung over the pews. Sam started down the aisle and slid on what looked like week-old cooked okra from somebody's garbage. The podium and pulpit chairs were all turned over on their sides. Lying open on the floor was the big Bible. Charcoal was smeared all over the Twenty-third Psalm.

Jeep must have stuffed half a box of Kleenex in her pockets that morning. She picked up the Bible and dabbed at the page easylike, but none of the smudge would come off "the house of the Lord forever."

Sam and I righted the pulpit and did all we could to clean up the rest of the mess. Then the three of us sat on the front pew to rest. Nobody talked. We had just about run out of words that were okay to say in church.

"My triply great grandpapa Joshua'd turn over two times in 'is grave to see such as this," Sam's voice sounded a shade mournful.

"What about the sheriff's men? Can't they do something?" I was thinking how the law was always snooping 'round Mirror Mountain.

"Yeah—what about them is right," Sam said. "Papa went to 'em for help. They said they'd try. Then

Sheriff Soames told 'im it was just too deep in the woods to come regular. 'E told Papa they were short-handed."

"Maybe they're scared of ghosts." Jeep folded her arms and raised her chin. "You know all those stories about the church being haunted."

Sam's eyes got narrow. "More likely, they don't think an old Gullah church is worth their time. Our church is more than a hundred years old."

"Well, it's more valuable because it is so old," Jeep said. "I bet Mrs. Lucretia wouldn't just sit here waiting for somebody else to do something."

She stood up and put her hands on her hips. "So why can't we be more like Mrs. Lucretia and stop all this vandalizing ourselves?"

"We who?" Sam wanted to know.

"You, me, and Johnny. We'll also need Louise."

I shook my head. "Four younguns, you mean. We just gonna come down here and face no telling how many dangerous punks. Why, they might even have knives or guns." I was thinking how I might not live to get back to Mirror Mountain or see Ma and Pa and Aunt Lou again. Then I thought of something else. "And there's Uncle Jake. Me and Louise got to look after him."

"Cool it, Johnny." Jeep looked straight in my eyes. "I don't mean for us to put ourselves in danger. We'll just find out who's doing it, then get the sheriff."

"And we won't expect you to neglect Mister Jake,"

34

said Sam. "Anyhow, you know 'is feelings 'bout this island and all its history."

"Yeah, he loves it, all right. He might start to get happy again if he knows we helped save the church." I took a deep breath. "Count me in, but we better don't tell the grown-ups what we got in mind."

"Not yet, anyhow," Sam agreed.

My stomach growled the time of day it was. "Hey, what you say we lock up and go home. It's time to eat."

I didn't get a lick of back talk over that suggestion.

# 5
# Gull Inlet Encounter

Our midday dinner was baked beans and green salad. Louise was cooking all our food without much grease or salt. That was how Sae Simmons said Uncle Jake was supposed to eat it. I didn't really mind. It was just that I sure could have gone for a piece of fried fatback on the side.

Sam's mama smiled a lot and never talked too loud. Her full name was Sarah, but everyone called her Sae, even Sam. She came by almost every day to check Uncle Jake's blood pressure. She reminded me of pictures I had seen of beautiful Indian princesses. Her long, blue-black hair was shiny like the back of a crow. She balled it up at the back of her neck and kept a curvy comb stuck in it.

When we started eating, I told Louise and Uncle Jake what we had run into at the church. Since he had seen fit to talk about that last night, I thought he might be interested.

"Uncle Jake, who do you think would mess up a

church like that?" I asked.

He shook his head. "Nobody with decent raisin' or reason. Preacher Abe don't and never did hurt nobody."

"Some people don't need a reason to be mean," Louise put in.

Nobody said anything else for a while. I started thinking of what else I could ask Uncle Jake, to make him talk more. Ma's uncle never talked about Aunt Mollie or Lester, I thought. It was too bad I didn't keep my thinking in my head.

"Uncle Jake, how come you keep Lester's room locked?" I blurted out.

Louise's mouth flew open. She stretched her eyes wide at me, and made a ring with her mouth. I hated when she did that. What I asked didn't seem all that wrong to me, so I kept going. "Why don't you ever open it, Uncle Jake?"

It pesters me how my sister's warnings turn out to be right so much of the time. Uncle Jake stiffened up like the hairs on the neck of a wild boar about to charge. His steely grey eyes glared pure hate at me. "Mind your own business, boy." His voice cut through me like a sharp knife. He stood up and shoved his chair back. It hit the floor with a loud WHAM. After that, his slippers scraped across the floor as he headed for his room. Then we heard his door bang shut.

Louise was still glaring at me. "I hope you're real proud of yourself," she snapped. "He didn't even finish his dinner."

"I ain't, am not proud," I shot back. "I was a'fixin' to ask him if he cared to go fishing today. I just asked him one dinky little question. He acts like I committed some crime."

"Johnny Elbert, just try and put yourself in his place. Think how you'd feel if you lost all your loved ones."

"How? I ain't never lost somebody close to me. But if I did, I hope I wouldn't act so peculiar."

Louise sighed. "You don't know how you'd act. But what's done is done. Leave it be for now and come wipe the dishes."

While we worked, I told her about our plans to solve the vandal mystery.

"Now don't you go blabbin' to Uncle Jake," I warned.

"Huh! Look who's talking." A tiny frown went over her face. "But we better be careful not to neglect or worry him. As for going after vandals, we need to organize. I've been reading mysteries. There's always clues to be investigated." She gasped, "Don't drop that glass, Johnny!"

"Oh, I won't." The glass I was drying had all but slid out of my hand. I was thinking that maybe Sam and I been out of our minds when we agreed to work with two bossy girls.

That thought had barely skimmed my brain when along came Jeep to side with Louise. She had ridden her bike over in the soppy afternoon heat.

"We'll have to meet and put together ideas and plans." Jeep had to stop a second to catch her breath. I couldn't help but notice how her short hair curled so pretty around her face. "Otherwise, we'll just run around in circles and get nothing done."

I told myself to watch out or those two girls would run circles 'round me. They were already taking charge, and I needed to get out of there. I was glad to hear Sam's Indian war whoop at the landing. Throwing the dish towel to Jeep, I let the screen door slam behind me.

Preacher Abe was in the *Chariot* and Sam sat by the motor.

"Papa says we can take a boat ride after we get 'im back to work," said Sam. "Get in, John E."

"WAIT FOR US!" It was the girls. Sam and I traded disgusted looks as Louise and Jeep came running down to the landing.

"Did you leave a note for Uncle Jake?" I barked at Louise.

"Of course. I'm not thoughtless like somebody else I know." She stuck out her tongue at me. The two girls climbed aboard and sat down at the front end of the boat.

"How y'all doing!" Preacher Abe said. He was a big man with a big voice that went with his big smile. Under his light blue shirt, you could see the muscles of his broad shoulders. He wore dark blue shorts that came to his knees. "Glad to have all of you aboard," he said. "Sam tells me you did a lot of work at the church this morning. I'm ever so much obliged for your helping 'im put things back to order."

"We didn't mind one bit," Jeep said. "It just seems the sheriff could do more to stop those vandals."

Preacher Abe straightened his glasses. He wore the kind that turned dark in the sunlight. "I'm gonna ask 'im again. The Bible says we're not to stop asking for the right things, you know. Luke 11, verse 9."

All of us fixed our eyes on his face. Our chins went up and down like hammers. Jeep took a little notebook out of her pocket. "Did you say verse 9?" Preacher Abe nodded and smiled, looking amply pleased that she was writing it down. I was surprised to see her making so much over Bible stuff. Aunt Lou would like Jeep for that.

Sam got the motor going. We moved out of the bay and through the green marshes of Gull Inlet. Great big water birds flapped out of the tall grass as the Chariot cut through the water, making little waves on both sides.

Soon we were passing docks and boat houses. Each dock was off the backyard of an expensive-looking house that faced the ocean. The row of big cottages stretched all the way to Wistero Beach.

We were not far from Gull Inlet Landing when a yellow speedboat pulled out from a little inlet and headed toward us. It was going real fast. Big spurts of water jetted out on each side of the boat as it kept coming straight at us. I didn't see how it was going to miss slamming into the *Chariot*. I looked at Preacher Abe and he wasn't smiling anymore. He was yelling into Sam's ear, and Sam wasn't smiling, either. The girls screamed.

Please don't let them hit us, I prayed.

# 6
# Vick and Kevin

The boat moved closer and closer till we could see it had two boys in it. One had long, yellow hair flying out behind him. The other one's hair was dark and curly. Both had deep tans and wore bright sports shirts. They were coming so fast I don't know how I noticed all that dumb stuff. My hands felt like they were glued onto the sides of my seat. The speedboat kept coming toward us without slowing down the least bit, and I just knew we were goners.

But I'm still here to tell it. In a split second, the yellow boat did swerve and miss us. It couldn't have been by more than an inch or two. My heart did flip-flops. Preacher Abe's "Praise the Lord" sounded like a sonic boom over the noise of the motors.

The curly haired guy waved back at the girls like he thought he was some kind of superhero.

"Downright irresponsible!" Preacher Abe almost shouted.

"That's Vick and Kevin, all right," Jeep said.

Sam hollered something that sounded like "stinkin' rich brats." By now, he had slowed down the *Chariot* and was steering it into the cove at Gull Inlet Landing.

Preacher Abe got out and pointed his finger at Sam. "Remember who you are, son," he scolded. "Christians don't have a right to put other people down with name-calling and such."

It was a good thing for me to hear just then. I wasn't thinking kindly towards those smart alecks that almost got us killed. It came to me that Preacher Abe was already praying for Vick and Kevin. If they were the ones trashing up Deepwood Church, he probably trusted God to put brakes on them, somehow.

After Preacher Abe left us, we decided to go to Conch Island and have our meeting there. I was glad we didn't run into Vick and Kevin on our way. There were lots of little inlets they might have come tearing out of.

Conch Island looked deserted. Uncle Jake had told us he wouldn't take more than five or six shell hunters over at one time. "Too many people spoil the beach," he said.

We put down our anchor in a little cove and pulled off our sneakers. The hills of sand that Sam called dunes were hot. We cooled our feet by wading in the suds the waves made. The Atlantic Ocean off the other side of the island was dark blue-green and the far-off sky seemed to touch the water.

Jeep had a tiny shell book along with the notebook

in her pocket. "I thought we'd see what came in on the noon tide," she explained.

We picked up some shells that were pictured in the book. Then Louise found a big, smooth log for us to sit on. Sam called it driftwood.

Without being asked, Jeep took charge. "First, we need to know what each person does best," she said.

"I notice little things other people miss," Louise spoke up to say.

"Ummmmm-hummh," I muttered aside to Sam.

Jeep was writing in her notebook. "Good, Louise." She threw me and Sam a hard schoolteacher look. "We all need to be alert for such clues," she told us.

"What we gonna call ourselves?" asked Sam, digging his long toes into the sand. Sam didn't seem to like meetings any more than I did.

"I'm glad you asked that question," she told him. Again, she wrote in her notebook. "Any suggestions from the floor?"

"Jeep, the beach ain't a floor," Sam came back. "Might we be the Litter Squad?"

Jeep said that name sounded too, too gross. Nobody else liked it, either. Everyone threw out more dumb names like Bay Crew, Church Mice, and the like. None of them seemed right.

Over the dunes behind us, the sound of a boat motor slowed, then stopped.

"Sounds like somebody's coming," Sam said. "Anybody else got any ideas?"

Now there was just the sound of waves swishing onto the shore and the blowing of breezes that smelled like the sea.

Then an idea hit me like one of those waves hitting the shore. "Vandal Busters!" I yelled.

"Yeahhhhh!" Everyone liked it, and Jeep printed our name in big letters in her notebook.

It didn't take long to organize our group. Sam was elected president, and they picked me for vice president. Jeep was already being the secretary. If any money had to be handled, Louise would do it.

"Now we got to talk about investigating two jerky dudes," Sam reminded us.

"Won't need to go far for that," said Louise. "Here they come over the dunes right now."

Sure enough, Vick and Kevin walked straight to where we sat like they had every right to. They wore bathing trunks under their big, expensive shirts. The sneakers on their feet had labels on them. Some of my schoolmates back at Cougarville made a big to-do about owning name-brand shoes. Not me. The ones my Pa can afford do just fine.

"Hi, Jeep," said the yellow-headed one. "Long time no see since last summer. Find anything good today?"

"Depends on what you think's good, Kevin," she cut back over her shoulder. "Running your speedboat too close to us was not cool, in case you're interested. It was just plain dumb."

He cocked his head like what she said might be

trying to find his brain. "I guess so. We're sorry." He looked at his curly haired pal. "Aren't we sorry, Vick?"

Vick nodded without smiling. "We promise not to do it again." He had his eye on Louise. My sister's not bad looking, though I'd eat dirt before telling her so. Her head is big enough already over how she plays the guitar and sings. I tell her she's got cat eyes. They're brown with yellow-red specks like sugar maple leaves in the fall. Her hair is pale gold like wheat, but I call it cattail fuzz to her face.

I looked at Sam. He was scowling. I would have to remind him to keep a lid on his feelings about those boys. I had noticed how TV detectives played along with suspects till they could nail them.

Jeep introduced Louise and me to the two boys. Vick stood near Louise asking questions about where we lived and the like. But Jeep and Kevin had their heads close together over that old shell book. It was purely sickening how he knew all the hard-to-say names of shells.

For once, I kept my mouth shut. These guys didn't seem so bad, after all. But I remembered how Pa used to say that people who acted too nice might bear watching.

"I've never seen Deepwood House up close," I heard Kevin say to Jeep.

"You could walk there from Deepwood Bay. Do you know where Bay Road is?"

"Not really."

Jeep gave him directions, then drew a little map for him to follow.

"Is it true what I've heard about a witch doctor living in the jungle?" Kevin asked.

"Yes, but she's not close to Bay Road. If you're scared of having a spell cast on you . . ." Jeep was fixing him with a devilish look. I took it for flirting, which I didn't care for.

"Who said I was scared?" Kevin smiled back at her. "I just heard all those stories they tell on the island." He turned to Sam. "I'll bet you know lots of 'em, Sam."

My friend stared hard at Kevin for a minute. "Maybe I do and maybe I don't." He stood up. "Tide's turning, guys. The *Chariot's* taking off right away. All that's going with me, come along now."

Vick and Kevin said they would hang around a little longer and look for shells. The rest of us followed Sam back over the dunes. While we pulled on our sneakers, we eyed the snazzy yellow speedboat. A mountain boy could only dream of owning a boat like that.

When we got back to Uncle Jake's landing, Louise said, "Those boys might be reckless, but I don't think they're the vandals."

"Neither do I," piped in Jeep.

"Just because they sweet-mouthed you girls?" Sam shook his head and straightened his cap. "Crooks know how to throw people off the track."

47

"Sam's right about that," I agreed.

I just happened to look at Jeep and she was looking at me. "We'll just play along with them till we're sure," she said. "I think those boys just need somebody to care about them, maybe get them going to church. Don't worry, Johnny. We'll find out soon enough if they aren't okay."

I didn't know why I was brushing back that pesky lock of hair again. It never stayed put. "M-maybe," I said. "But there's just one way to find out. We got to stake the church at night."

"You said it, man!" Sam came back.

"I don't know," Louise said. "Uncle Jake wouldn't want . . ."

"Uncle Jake'll be snoring by sundown," I reminded her.

She agreed that from suppertime on, we wouldn't be missed. Most likely, Uncle Jake wouldn't wake up till morning.

"So far, the vandals have come on Friday or Saturday," Sam said. "It ain't like we got to go every night. My folks turn in early, too." He shrugged his shoulders. "Then I stay in my room till all hours, drawing pictures."

"No problem here, either," Jeep said. "When Dad's at that word processor, he doesn't know if the sun's shining by day or the moon by night. There's a big-limbed oak by my window. I'll climb down and wait for you in the shrubbery by the road."

"Okay, but wear long jeans and dark tops!" Sam started the motor and waved as the *Chariot* headed north. Soon it went out of sight around the palmettos and myrtles that hid the Simmonses' house from Uncle Jake's.

# 7
# Stakeout

"Uncle Jake wouldn't even look at me tonight," I told Louise after he went to his room.

"I noticed. But don't you go feeling too guilty, Johnny Elbert. Even if your tongue wags off its hinges, it ain't, isn't all your fault. Sae says he's got his hurts locked inside him. You just turned 'em loose for a spell, and he's hurtin' worse."

"Me too. I wish I was back on Mirror Mountain. Another day's over and there's still no mail from home."

"Maybe they're expecting mail from *us*. Did you write Ma and Pa yet? Or Aunt Lou?"

"I been aiming to."

"Well, you'd better get busy and do it. And don't you go whining to them about being homesick. They don't need to hear nothing but happy stuff."

"Louise, I didn't have a bit of mind to write nothing but happy stuff. How come you're all the time puttin' me down? You don't say them hurtful things to other people. Just me."

"Other people's not my brother." I reckon she

figured that made sense.

I was glad Louise didn't go into how rotten I was at writing anything. I couldn't spell worth a hoot. With Sandy McRee tutoring me, I had managed to get promoted, but Louise was skipping a grade. The school wouldn't let me do that. First, I had to do better on reading and writing. Now I was sorry the judge didn't order a little bus to come up Mirror Rock Road sooner. It was hard trying to make up the three years we missed because we didn't have a way to school.

After we had finished in the kitchen, Louise and I changed our clothes. I could hear Uncle Jake snoring when I went to the bathroom. He snored loud, but not too loud for me to hear a little noise in Lester's room. I put my ear to the wall on that side of the bathroom. Nothing. Maybe it was just my imagination.

Louise and I locked all the doors from the inside except the screen door nearest my cot. With our heads wrapped up in dark blue bandanas, we looked like pirates when we met Sam under the big oak.

We found Jeep where she said she would be. She had some pieces of charcoal for us to rub on our faces. Sam said he'd pass on that. I tried to rub some on him anyway. I kept going after him and he kept ducking away from me.

"If you boys can't be quieter, we don't need you," Louise warned.

I wondered what they might do in that scary place

without me and Sam. But I didn't want to know. It was more fun to picture them running after us, helpless and afraid.

The moon was full, so we didn't need flashlights to walk with. Going down the church lane, we hunkered next to big tree trunks. A little breeze shook the gray moss. I thought about the island spirits that were said to fly with feet turned backwards, blowing down air that was both hot and chilly at the same time. Of course I knew all that was just superstition. No matter. Just knowing Voodoo Boone lived somewhere out in the jungle gave me the willies.

From then on, we were quiet as we knew how to be until we were sure the church was deserted. This time Sam thought to bring the key. The door made a loud squeak when he opened it. "Got to remember to oil the hinges," Sam whispered.

Inside, we turned on our flashlights and crept down the aisle. The walls creaked, and I was glad nobody could see me shiver.

"Now," said Jeep, "we need to split up. Two inside and two in the yard."

"I'm the president," snapped Sam. "I decide."

Jeep held out her hands and bowed to him. "Yes, Chief Samuel. But hurry." All of us waited for him to hurry.

Sam stood tall as he flashed his light on the electric organ in the choir loft. There was a short, red velvet curtain around the loft. "Just stoop down between that curtain and the organ," Sam said.

"We can do that," piped Louise as they slipped under the curtain.

I ignored my sister's sassy tone. "Sam," I said, "us boys better stay close by the church. And girls, don't you scream less'n the vandals find you."

"We'll be quiet as church mice," Jeep promised. The sound of giggles broke out from behind the curtain.

"That's right, girls." Sam's tone was snotty. "Just keep on giggling and them vandals gonna git you for certain."

When we went outside, he turned to me. "You climb up in the big magnolia, John E. I'll hide in the bushes next the church where you can see me."

"And if somebody comes? We gotta have a plan, Sam."

"Right. Till they start something, don't do nothing. First one to see they didn't come here for praisin' the Lord, give a loud Indian whoop. Then we shine our lights right in the dudes' faces. Got to identify 'em, you know."

"Then what we gonna do?"

"Whatever we have to, I reckon." Sam didn't go on to say what that might be. I had my own ideas, and they did not slow down my breathing.

From the magnolia tree, I could hear safe night sounds, water flowing in the little well, crickets chirping and whippoorwills calling.

There was a sudden rustle in the leaves above my head. I nearly fell out of the tree. Were vandals watching us? I didn't move a muscle, thinking what I might do if one dropped down on top of me. After a couple of seconds passed, a low, round whoolooh sounded. I stretched my neck and looked up. Against the moonlight in the leaves, I made out the shape of an owl. I closed my eyes and sighed with relief.

No sound came from the church. It seemed like we had waited a long, long time. I wondered how much longer the four of us could keep still and quiet.

Nothing happened. Maybe they won't come tonight, I thought. When I was ready to say we ought to give it up, the critter noises stopped.

A different kind of sound came from the jungle. Heavy footsteps crashed through the bushes. Closer and closer. It was like a giant's walk might sound when he was too lazy to pick up his feet. My heart speeded up again. I could hear it pounding out the beats like it might break through my chest.

I pointed my nose toward the sound. A figure came out of the shadows. It wasn't tall enough to be a giant, but the creep was bundled up in some kind of floppy wrap and dragged something heavy behind him. I swallowed. The ghostlike thing stopped about ten feet from my tree. I held my breath. Was it a man with a gun? Then I remembered what I had to do. I aimed my flashlight straight at the figure. I tried to balance on the limb so I could turn on the flashlight with one hand while I used the other hand for the Indian whoop.

Before I could push the button on my flashlight, a weird roar sounded from inside the church. Another long drawn-out sound followed. The organ! Straight off I got the light on and gave the loudest wildcat yell I could.

Sam tore out of the bushes with a fierce holler. I got the quickest kind of look at the thing's face. It had a stocking over it like bank robbers on TV. There was no way to tell what the face really looked like. The thing dropped whatever it was dragging and took to the jungle faster than a race runner skink being chased by a copperhead moccasin.

"After 'im!" Sam bellowed, bouncing out of the bushes.

I scrambled to the ground. "Don't be stupid, Sam. You know that boggy woods ain't no place for us to be tearing 'round at night."

Jeep and Louise came tumbling down the steps, and Sam was plenty teed off at them. "We told you to be quiet!"

"We couldn't help what happened," Jeep explained. "I accidently leaned against the switch."

"And I didn't know it was on," added Louise. "I was just touching the organ keys for fun." Talking out of their charcoal faces, they looked like two bad little girls caught stealing cookies.

"No use getting hot under the collar," I told Sam.

"We saw as much of his face as we could have, anyway."

Jeep caught her nose. "Something smells terrible."

"It's in that sack he dropped." I went over with Sam to look in it.

The only thing that could have smelt worse was skunk. It was a huge fish, dead and mushy rotten.

"What an ingenuous way to stink up the church for tomorrow's service," Jeep said, still holding her nose.

"Are you gonna tell Preacher Abe?" I asked Sam.

"Of course not. We can't let nobody know we been here tonight. We got to get rid of the stinking fish."

We didn't have a shovel, so we dragged the smelly sackful down the road apiece and threw it in the woods. People might smell it going to church, but at least they wouldn't smell it while they worshiped.

Just before we got to Deepwood House, a car surprised us from behind. A second car followed the first one. We ducked in the bushes real quick and watched both of them turn into the drive ahead of us.

"That was Sherman Attaway's little foreign bug in front," Jeep said. "Wonder who was in the other one?"

"A new renter, I s'pose," Sam said. "Let's just hope 'e didn't see us good enough to tell who we were."

Uncle Jake was still snoring when we got home.

When I went to the bathroom, I heard the noise in Lester's room again. Not a loud noise, but something rattling around. I got back to the dining room fast.

Louise looked at me and smiled. "You heard it, too,

56

huh? It's probably just mice."

She had set out Aunt Mollie's old sewing basket on the table and was busy taking up Uncle Jake's pajama pants. "I'm too keyed up to sleep yet," she said.

I wasn't sleepy, either. I found some notebook paper and a pencil. Sitting across from Louise, I tried to write to Ma and Pa. But all I could think of was what I couldn't put in a letter, going after vandals and how bad things had got between me and Uncle Jake.

# 8
# Shades of Voodoo Boone

"Johnny Elbert, I don't see how you can sleep with the sun a'shining in your face."

"Beat it, Louise."

My sister had just washed her hair and had it hanging over to dry in the sunny breeze on the porch. She kept shaking her head like a wet dog. "It's Sunday, little brother. Didn't I tell you we're going to Deepwood Church?"

I groaned and let my feet flop to the floor. For a minute or so, I sat and scratched my head. "Why?"

"Because we got asked, that's why. Preacher Abe told me to bring my guitar. Sae says to try to talk Uncle Jake into coming, too."

I thought about the dusty Bible on the shelf in Uncle Jake's sleeping porch. "Ma told me he went to church at Wistero Beach."

"I know, but Sae told me he hadn't been there since—you know—the funerals. She said he and Aunt Mollie and Lester visited at Deepwood Church once or twice before that." She gave her hair a heavy sweep with the hairbrush. "Get moving, Johnny. I'll take Uncle Jake his medicine. Pancakes are ready to pour on the griddle."

Breakfast was worth hurrying for. I told Louise I'd fix Uncle Jake's pancakes while she tended to our dinner on the stove. She had boiled a chicken Saturday morning, and now she was cooking rice with it.

For the first time since we got there, Uncle Jake came to breakfast. He acted like he didn't see me flipping pancakes for him. I figured if I showed him I could do little things right, he might decide I could also do the big things, like running his boat to Conch Island. I just couldn't give up wanting to do that.

When he finished a second helping with syrup poured on, Ma's depressed uncle looked as contented as a fly on a pie.

"Uncle Jake, we sure could use a ride to church," Louise said. "And Sae said she hoped you might come and visit, too."

We could have waited at the big oak by the mailboxes to catch a ride with the Simmonses. But Louise said Jeep was going with us, and that would be too many people in one car. I knew it was my sister's way of making Uncle Jake feel we needed him to drive us.

He got up and squinted at the bay. "I reckon I'll go along and drive you. The old Chevy needs to be cranked up once in a while."

I felt like saying his car wasn't all that needed cranking, but didn't. My big mouth had already outdone itself with Uncle Jake.

When he came out dressed for church, I thought glory be! He looked more like his old self in a light green shirt and tan pants. Louise was all perked up in a flowered dress and sandals. I wore new jeans and a shirt I got for my birthday.

Uncle Jake's old Chevy leaned to one side and its grey paint was peeling off. I was surprised when the engine turned over the first time he tried it.

Jeep was waiting for us in front of Deepwood House. I had never seen her in a dress before. The one she wore was a purplish color that matched her eyes, and her sandals were purple, too.

Like Louise, she had brought a little Bible along. I didn't have mine with me. It was still in my duffel bag. Aunt Lou would say that was a fine howdy do for a boy who had made Jesus his Lord and got baptized.

Jeep slid into the backseat next to Louise and her old guitar. "It's great to have a ride," she told Uncle Jake. As we moved on, she said, "My mom and I never missed church when she was living. Dad goes with me sometimes, but down here, he's been so busy writing that book, he doesn't know Sunday from any other day."

"When did you lose your mother?" Louise asked.

"Two years ago. I still miss her. She was always helping other people and leading them to the Lord.

That's one reason I like to help people. It makes me feel close to her and not so sad." She said all that real fast, then bit her lip when she finished.

I cut my eye at Uncle Jake to see if he heard what Jeep said. He was just staring straight ahead. I was sitting right next to him, and I could just as well have been floating in the Atlantic Ocean for all the notice he paid me. I was glad when we got to the church.

Sae, in a yellow dress, stood at the foot of the steps with Preacher Abe. He looked great in black and white. We could hear the happy smile in his voice before it got to his face. And we saw every tooth in his jaw when Jeep said, "I looked up Luke 11:9. It says just what you told us it did, Preacher Abe."

Louise played her guitar to sing a solo. Then everybody did a lot of singing. In our church on the mountain, we sang lots of gospel songs. Right off, we found out these folks did, too. Soon the place was full of singing with hand clapping and foot stomping.

Uncle Jake was the only one who didn't sing. He sat there like he dared anybody to pry open his mouth. But I noticed the toes of his shoes wiggling when everyone got happy singing "on my way to heaven, I shall not be moved."

I wondered what Jeep thought of how the people worshiped. I had heard that some of the city churches have books that say when to stand, sit, pray, or sing, but Jeep was doing just fine with no book. She sang and clapped. When everyone prayed out loud at the same time, Jeep moved her lips and closed her eyes. I shut mine tight and prayed that Uncle Jake would stop being so hard to get along with.

When we got done praying, Preacher Abe said how glad he was we could visit. He thanked Louise for helping with the music. "Whatever might come against us," he went on to say, "we still worship in the church our ancestors built. Ohhh, my friends, we have been sorely tempted to sell. The offer, as you know, was more than enough to build a fine new church. But we have passed the test, brothers and sisters. We stand together for keeping our Lord's house like it's always been. Hallelujah!" He raised both hands, and the people did, too.

"Amen. You tell 'em, Preacher Abe!" said a man just behind us. The others mumbled agreement.

Then Preacher Abe stretched himself even taller than he was already. "THIS IS THE DAY THAT THE LORD HATH MADE. LET US REJOICE AND BE GLAD IN IT!"

"Hallelujah. Yeah. Lord made it." A white-haired man in the second row waved both hands. All around us people waved their hands and shouted "Praise the Lord!"

The sermon was from I Corinthians, chapter 13. It was about loving each other like God told us to, even if we don't get loved back. Nobody went to sleep during the service. They were too busy agreeing with Preacher Abe.

We were the only visitors. Before the closing prayer, Preacher Abe asked the congregation to wait for us to go out front with him and Sae and Sam. He wanted the congregation to get a chance to shake our hands.

But it didn't go the way he planned. On the front steps, somebody had left a cloth doll dressed in black and white just like Preacher Abe. Sharp little sticks were pushed into the doll.

Sae caught hold of Sam's arm. "Get rid of this before any of the congregation sees it," she ordered.

One look at Sae's face was all it took. Sam yanked the doll and headed for the jungle. The rest of the Vandal Busters ran after him.

Under two big pines, Sam pulled the sticks out of the doll. He pitched it to the ground like it was a hot potato. "I s'pose you know what this heah is?" He gave it a quick stomp with his foot.

"Voodoo Boone's calling card." Jeep glared at Sam. "Now do you think Vick and Kevin are the vandals?"

"I'm not ready to rule 'em out, Jeep. You'd be surprised, the kind of people messin' with witchcraft these days."

"And Kevin reads lots of books," I put in, cutting my eye at Jeep. "Both of 'em got the money to buy what books they want."

Louise just stood there looking down at the doll. "Voodoo Boone sews neat seams." She shivered. "I don't think I could jab sticks in something I took such pains to make just so."

Jeep nodded. "One thing is positive. We have another suspect to investigate."

I agreed, but the idea didn't set easy. Uncle Jake's gory tales about the witch doctor spooked my brain. I was all for piling straw on top of the doll and making a beeline back to the churchyard, which we did.

Going home, Jeep said she and her dad were going to Charleston for what she called lunch. "Then he wants to stop by the library to do some research. We'll be late getting home."

Sam had already told me his family was invited to a picnic dinner and church meeting on another island. We didn't get a chance to plan for the next move of the Vandal Busters.

Back home, we had just finished our dinner of chicken bog and green salad when Uncle Jake said, "I'm wore out," then started for his room.

"It was sure nice of you to drive us this morning, Uncle Jake." Louise sounded like Ma talking.

He turned before going through the door and almost smiled. "Much obliged, Louise. That was mighty good bog you fixed for dinner." He didn't say one word about the green salad I had put together.

Louise's eyes were shiny the way they get when she's pleased with herself. "It's like Sae said, Johnny. We have to be patient. She says if we just show love to Uncle Jake, God will do the healing."

I wanted to believe he was getting better. I wanted

to show I loved Ma's uncle, too. But right then, I wasn't sure I even liked him.

That afternoon Louise curled up in a big wooden chair on the shady porch to read a book.

A nice little breeze cooled me as I sat on my cot. I got out the letter I started the night before and finished it. I didn't bother to look up words. Ma and Pa didn't spell good, either.

Dear Ma and Pa and Aunt Lou,
We are fine. Uncle Jake drove us to church today. The ocean is miety big and purty. I hope you write soon. I miss you. Yours Truly, Johnny

Ma had packed stamps in my duffel bag, but I had to empty it to find them. I dumped everything on my cot.

My Living Bible fell out and I thought about Jeep. Pa had given me the Bible when I joined the church. I decided right then that I was going to start reading it every day. I found Luke 11:9.

The words were easy to read: "And so it is with prayer—keep on asking and you will keep on getting; keep on looking and you will keep on finding; knock and the door will be opened."

I turned to chapter 13 of I Corinthians, and read all of it. Some of the words I had to sound out and didn't understand. Verses 4 and 5 said things about love that made me wonder if I had it in me to act like a Christian ought to act. It said love hardly even notices

65

when others do wrong things. I didn't understand that much at all.

I stuck my face in my pillow and prayed, "Lord, how can I not notice? I let You stand tall in me. That's how I done lots of things I thought I couldn't. I got up 'fore all of Cougarville Elementary and talked about wild herbs. I stood up to Aunt Lou when she said she didn't need me sleeping at her house at night. But it sure looks like I've just plain blown it with Uncle Jake. Like You said to, I'm beggin' in the name of Jesus."

I lay still on my stomach for a spell. It was real quiet except for the gulls and egrets calling over Deepwood Bay. It might have been I just dozed off and dreamed it. But under my eyelids, that last verse jumped out of the dark at me. I saw every word just like I read it.

"There are three things that remain—faith, hope, and love—and the greatest of these is love."

Wow!

# 9
# Anyone for Conch Island?

The next morning, Sae picked up Uncle Jake to drive him to Charleston. It was time for his checkup with the heart doctor. Sam tagged along to visit some cousins who lived on the way to the medical center.

The minute the Dodge rolled out of sight, Louise said, "I'm gonna clean Uncle Jake's room while he's gone. Honest to goodness, Johnny, men don't never disturb dust. Now, I don't need you to help. Just stay in hollering distance."

"Uncle Jake's not gonna like you disturbing his stuff."

"He's bound to like a cleaner room."

Just watching Louise on one of her cleaning sprees plumb wears me out. In no time, she was singing and stirring up dust in Uncle Jake's room. I'm here to tell you, this mountain boy needed space. I got my cricket cage and fishing pole.

Some time before we came, a hurricane had knocked a great big tree over into the bay. At low tide, it made a super place to sit and fish. But today my eyes lit on Uncle Jake's boat. Now, with him gone to Charleston, what harm could come if I paddled it around the edge of the bay? I was bound to find better fishing places that way.

I went to the boat house for a paddle and took a notion to practice the checklist Sam had written out for me. I kept it handy in my jeans pocket, but pretty much knew it by heart.

First, I put life cushions and paddles into the boat. Next, I unscrewed the top of the gas tank. It was half full, so I went back for the jug of gasoline and filled it. Uncle Jake would have been surprised at how careful I was not to spill any gas. I put the jug back in exactly the same place I had found it.

I sat in the boat beside the motor and pulled the brim of my old straw hat over my face. I hated that old tacky hat. I wanted a baseball cap like Sam's real bad. Maybe Ma would send some money so I could buy myself one. There were lots of them at the shop next to the post office at Wistero Beach. But like everything else on the island, they cost too much.

I paddled out a few feet and stabbed a big, fat cricket with my hook. Then I set the pole out deeper in the water. As I waited for something to jiggle my cork, I heard a car coming through the jungle.

I'm built so my head just sits on my shoulders. When I turn it, the rest of me gets a good twist, too. I watched a spanking new Oldsmobile ease into the clearing and stop. A white-haired man got out first. Then three younguns tumbled from the car, with a blue-eyed lady close behind them. I could tell these folks hadn't been long on the island. Their beach clothes looked too new and their skin was too white. They had plastic milk jugs with the fronts cut out above the handles.

The man's friendly smile made me think he might be a preacher. Or maybe a politician.

"Good morning!" Even his voice had a smile in it. "How much would you charge for taking us and our grandchildren to Conch Island?" He asked.

I pushed my hat back off my face. I knew that Uncle Jake's way of making up tours had been to turn on his phone late in the afternoon. It stayed on only till he had set up what trips could be taken during low tide the next day. Of course, his phone had been off ever since we came.

The man was so nice, I just hated to tell him Uncle Jake didn't do tours anymore. There they were, not asking if I could take them, but how much I charged for the trip.

I reckon I forgot where pretending was supposed to stop. "Three dollars apiece for one hour on the island, sir!" I was already paddling back to where they waited.

They were all sitting in the boat ready to travel when it barely skidded over my brain that maybe I shouldn't go through with this. But quicker than you could say "curlin' rattlesnakes," I had the motor going.

I knew the sound would bring Louise to the porch, yelling for me to stop. I couldn't hear her above the motor, so I acted like I didn't see her at all. In no time, the boat was on its way. The children kept waving back at me, squealing and laughing. The woman had a nice smile, but the man whooped and hollered like he might be a youngun, too.

When we got to Conch Island, I eased the boat into the landing and tied it. While the family walked down the beach picking up shells, I waded in the bubbly suds. Tiny coquina clams wiggled in shells that looked like nervous butterflies. When the water went away, they tickled my feet as they dived into the wet sand.

The sound of wind and waves curled 'round the happy shouts of the youngsters. "Look what I found, Grandpa Joe!"

"Beautiful," he called back, and I could tell it didn't matter what they found; he just plain loved his grandchildren. It took me back to when I was a little boy. Just then, I wanted to holler "Look at me!" loud enough for Ma and Pa and Aunt Lou to hear me all the way from Mirror Mountain.

When it was time to leave, they were all singing

"This is the day, this is the day that the Lord has made," and so on. If he wasn't a preacher, I figured the man knew the Lord right well.

All the time I was in charge of that boat, I didn't once feel I had done anything wrong by taking those folks to hunt shells. When we got back to the landing, the man paid me $15 and said "you're a good boat pilot, er . . ."

"Johnny Elbert Finlay," I said. "I'm glad you had a good time, mister."

"The name is McFaddin. My wife and I will certainly tell our friends how much fun we've had this morning. God bless you, Johnny Elbert." We shook hands and they took off in the Olds.

Before I stuffed the money in my jeans pocket, I thought how it might be enough for the cap I wanted. Then it came to me to consider whose boat I had taken out without permission. It wasn't my money. It was Uncle Jake's, and I had to figure out some way to see that he got it.

I made sure the boat was tied up, put the gear away, and came out of the boat house feeling a foot taller. Then I looked up and saw my sister. She stood over me like a mountain lookout tower.

"Get out of my face, Louise!" I bellowed. I tried to stare her down. The girl would not budge.

"Johnny Elbert, you are the most stubborn Finlay of all the stubborn Finlays that ever lived," she declared. "First, you complain about Uncle Jake being upset with you. Then you go right out and disobey him."

I showed her the $15 I'd earned. "Maybe he'll change his mind when he sees this."

Louise stared at the two bills. "I wouldn't count on it."

"I won't tell him till he's in the right mood. You ain't, aren't gonna blab on me, are you?"

She sighed. "I will if he asks, knucklehead. Just stop being such a worry. Now you better make sure you put his money in a safe place, you hear?"

Before I could think of how to answer, a boat motor sounded from the mouth of Gull Inlet. The *Chariot* came swashing up to the landing.

"Mailman!" Preacher Abe called. He put down his anchor and stepped ashore. Preacher Abe tended the mailboxes under the big oak where Bay Road ended. Even Deepwood House had a box there.

"We put a letter in our box to go," I told him. We had offered to carry mail from the boxes to the boat. Preacher Abe said thanks, but he couldn't allow that. He was sworn to do it himself, no matter how much he trusted others. Before heading for the boxes, he handed Louise an envelope postmarked Cougarville, South Carolina. Inside were two letters. One for Louise, and one for me.

We read them soon as Preacher Abe left for dinner at his house. Then we went in to eat leftover chicken bog with sweet cucumber pickles and sliced tomatoes.

After dinner we both read our letters again. There wasn't much news. Ma said they missed us and hoped we were doing our best to get Uncle Jake well. Then she said they loved me, and Aunt Lou sent her love, too. Each letter had a five-dollar bill tucked in it.

I put my five with Uncle Jake's fifteen dollars and stuck all of it under the mattress of my cot on the screened porch. Then I went back to help Louise with the dishes.

Sam and Sae rode up right after we finished in the kitchen.

"I left your uncle in the hospital overnight for some tests the doctor wanted to do," Sae told us. "There's no cause for alarm. It's just routine stuff to be sure everything's all right. You youngsters can spend the night at our house if you'd like."

"Thanks, but we'll be fine here," Louise said.

"Well, we're there if you need us." Sae turned to Sam. "If you plan to use the *Chariot* this afternoon, we'd better get on home. I can give your papa a ride back to the post office." She headed for their silver blue Dodge.

Sam stood in the doorway till Sae was out of earshot. "We gonna cruise up the river," he said in a low voice. "I phoned Jeep this morning. She's bringing a cooler of lemonade."

"I'll make up some sandwiches," offered Louise.

"Good girl, Looo-weese!" Sam clapped his hands easylike. "The kind of brew Voodoo Boone might be

73

cookin' up might not be too appetizing." He raised his chin, wrinkled his nose and crossed his eyes. When we laughed, he crossed his chest with his hands and bowed to each of us in turn. A car horn sounded.

"Samuel Hezekiah Simmons, are you coming with me?" Sae called from car.

"Right now, your majesty!" he yelled. With a quick wave, he jogged away from us.

# 10
# Cruisin'
# Up the River

The whole idea of spying on Voodoo Boone gave me the creeps, but I was just dying to know what there was to all I had heard. How did the old witch doctor used dried frogs, snakes, lizards, and black cats in her brews? Did she heal ailments with the same gory stuff she used to cast spells and lay curses on people?

Sandy McRee had warned me that the Lord didn't want my brain plugged into any kind of power but His own. Preacher Abe taught the same. But it wasn't like we were going there for any of that hocus-pocus stuff. We were just Vandal Busters trying to save God's house.

Sam steered the *Chariot* past the Simmonses'

landing and through green marshes to the river. He had on a big red T-shirt with a widemouthed shark on it. He grinned real big when Jeep said it looked gross.

We got to the North Wistero River and motored against the current. The water got darker, and cypress knees stuck up along the edges of the river. After we had gone through that for a mile or two, Sam pulled out of the current and cut off the motor. "Get a paddle," he told me.

It didn't take long for me to see why we couldn't use the motor anymore. We paddled under some low-hanging willows and down a little stream. Looking ahead, the swamp we were in was like a mossy cave the boat crawled through. All around us, big spiders on cypress knees scooted out of sight. Chips of sunlight pushed through the leaves and lit up the white sand under the dark water. When a big, shiny snake slid off a log, its wriggly shadow looked like two snakes swimming side by side.

I never saw so many huge mosquitoes looking for a meal. They went through our repellent like it was red-eye gravy on ham. Slapping at them was a comfort Sam and I couldn't enjoy for having to do the paddling.

I do believe that girls would rather swallow mosquitoes than stop talking. It was plain that Jeep was just dying to tell us something.

"Strange things are going on at Deepwood House," she said. "Just before I left this afternoon, I saw

Sherman Attaway and Slag Hatton arguing under my window." She ducked under a low-hanging limb.

"Maybe old Sherman was dressin' Slag down about 'is sloppy work." Sam freed one hand from his paddle long enough to smash the blood out of a mosquito that had latched onto his ear.

Jeep shook her head. "I don't think Sherman cares what kind of work Slag does. I heard him say, 'Time's short. You got to get their attention.'"

"Whose attention?" It was hard to swat mosquitoes, paddle 'round cypress knees, and listen all at the same time. But no one wanted to miss what she was saying now.

"That's what I didn't hear, Johnny. They were under a tree where a mockingbird has a nest. The bird kept swooping down at them till they moved." She made a half-circle with her arms to show how the bird zipped down and back up. "Then Sherman came to the apartment across the hall from us where Mr. Barnes is staying. Remember the car that was following Sherman's little foreign bug Saturday night?"

"Yeah, yeah. Go on, Jeep." Sam was getting impatient.

"Well, I asked Irene Slatton about it, and she told me it's a rented car. She said Mr. Barnes had business with Sherman."

"Get to the point, Jeep," Louise urged. "What kind of business?" Sam and I stopped paddling to listen.

"Irene said she didn't know, that it was none of her

business or mine. If there had been time, I would have gone up on the widow's walk."

Louise sprayed some repellent on her hand and dabbed it on her neck. "What's that got to do with it?"

"There's a chimney over Mr. Barnes's sitting room. If you take the cover off, you can hear what's said in there. The first time I noticed was last summer. Two women had the apartment. They kept talking about how good looking my dad is." She giggled.

"I'd like to go up on that widow's walk," Louise said, smiling.

"You can. If you guys want, we'll have our next meeting there."

"All right," said Sam, "but till then, try to find out all you can 'bout what's goin' on. Maybe it has something to do with our case."

"I'll keep my eyes and my ears open," Jeep promised.

We went back to our paddling and the stream got wider. Then we came to a little pond. The water was still except for shadows of low-hanging moss that shivered above it. Up ahead I could see a creepy-looking shack in the trees.

A chill ran through me. Nobody had to say a thing. It had to be Voodoo Boone's house.

A low fence made out of crooked limbs went round what yard there was. Plastic milk bottles and shiny aluminum pie plates were strung along the fence.

"They're supposed to keep evil spirits away," Sam explained.

Jeep fixed him with a devilish look. "Really, Sam? I thought maybe she was just recycling."

"Funny, funny girl." He craned his long neck every which way, trying to see. "Don't look like she's home. What you say we go snooping?"

He stepped ashore under a weeping willow. I tailed him and helped pull the boat clear of the muddy bank. The girls had stopped talking. They looked scared, and I didn't feel so brave myself.

We got past the fence and up to the front door. It had a lock on it. Ragged shutters were over the windows, but we could see through the cracks. Sam was right—nobody was home. Inside was nothing but gloom, darker than Aunt Lou's root cellar. Herbs and roots hung from rafters in the ceiling, and the walls looked like they had always been midnight black.

"What's all that black cloth over the mirrors?" Louise asked.

Sam looked. "Uh-oh," he said. "That's old-time Gullah ways. Papa told me the old folks in our church still cover up the mirrors and pictures when somebody dies. They stop the clocks, too."

"Well, I can't see a clock, but it looks like somebody must have died," Jeep decided.

The ashes were cold under an old wash pot in the yard. It was empty and looked like it had been that way for some time. No dried frogs or snakes or spiders. A few feet away, the backyard joined up with the swamp.

"Where could she be?" Louise wondered.

Then I heard paddles sloshing in the little pond. I'm here to tell you, I wanted out of that place.

"What you younguns doin' at my auntie's house?" It was a woman's voice, talking loud. Voodoo Boone?

I looked at Sam. His eyes were big and round. Cold chills ran up my spine like something terrible was reaching out to grab me. Then I saw where the voice came from.

A woman was walking toward us, and a boy about my size was tying up a small canoe near the *Chariot*. The woman was tall, with big bony arms and legs. In half a minute she stood in front of us, hands on her hips. One by one, she just about stared a hole through each scared Vandal Buster.

"Y-You're not Maum Beulah," Sam stammered.

"More'n you be, I bet." The woman had a huffy voice and eyes as suspicious as a hungry cat's. "We the only livin' kin. Done buried 'er yesterday in 'er chosen place 'cross the river."

"I-I-we're sorry. When did she die?" Sam was acting braver than I felt.

"Two days ago. My Tony and me come from 'cross the river when we heah she was dying. Gonna close up this old nothin' of a house now. We gonna get home 'fore dark. I cared 'bout my Aunt Beulah, but never could go along with all that voodoo stuff. You still ain't answered my question."

"Oh. We were just riding around and happened up here," said Jeep.

"But we're gonna leave right now," I added in a hurry.

The woman shrugged. "Better do that. This no place for nobody to hang out. Me, I can't get away quick enough." She started toward the ugly little shack. "I don't itch to go back in there now, with all them covered-up mirrors and pictures."

The boy never opened his mouth to even say howdy. He just stood and stared after us as we paddled away. He looked scared, and I was sorry we couldn't ask him to go with us.

As we moved toward the river, Louise told Jeep she might as well strike Voodoo Boone from our suspect list.

"It's so awful," said Jeep. "That poor old woman dying in that dreary place."

Louise shook her head. "And trusting in milk cartons and pie plates to protect her."

In my mind, I could still see the crooked fence with its ghostlike hangings. My sweat turned cold and clammy just thinking about it.

I know the Bible says "perfect love drives out fear," but I figure it also helps to eat something. We stopped at the edge of the river. Not one crumb of Louise's peanut butter and jelly sandwiches nor a drop of Jeep's lemonade got thrown to the fishes.

The *Chariot* pulled in at the Simmonses' landing about the same time Preacher Abe and Sae got home from work.

Sam didn't tell Preacher Abe we had been to Maum Beulah's. He just said a woman in a boat had told us the old witch doctor was dead. That was no lie, but it was just part of the truth.

Preacher Abe shook his head. "If only I could have won Maum Beulah to the Lord." He looked sad about that.

Sae put her hand on his shoulder. "Don't be so hard on yourself, Abe. Voodoo Boone never let health workers help her, either. Just think of all the souls that will be in heaven because they did let you help, honey."

Jeep looked sad. "I'd like to win someone to the Lord," she said. "I never have. Do you think God might use me to do that, Preacher Abe?"

Sam's papa looked at Jeep in such a kind, gentle way. "Honey, if the Lord put that desire in your heart, He will sure enough carry you the rest of the way. Just . . ."

"I know," Jeep cut in. "Just keep on asking."

Preacher Abe smiled and nodded.

After we had unloaded the *Chariot* and put up the gear, Preacher Abe told us the sheriff had come by the post office that day. "Somebody reported seeing some black children on Bay Road Saturday night. Near the church," he told us.

I wouldn't look at anyone. At first, nobody said a

thing. Then I heard Sam clear his throat. "They did, Papa?"

"That's what he said. I told him the church wasn't hit that night. It was probably just some young folks walking in the moonlight. You know, from the neighborhood down beyond the forks." He looked at me and Louise. "Most of our church families live there."

"That's a long way for them to walk," Sae said.

"Not for those young athletes. They jog for miles. Anyhow, secondhand reports aren't too reliable."

We just nodded. Then Louise said we ought to get back and check on the house before dark. I was glad she thought of that excuse to get away right then.

After Jeep left for Deepwood House on her bike, Louise and I sat on the screened porch. She tuned up her guitar, twisting the knobs, her ear close to the strings. "I don't feel right, Johnny," she said. We should've told Preacher Abe it was us there on Bay Road."

"Louise, you know if we'd done that, he would've told us we couldn't go stake out the church no more. The Vandal Busters can't quit now."

"Well, at least we know it's not Voodoo Boone, and I..."

A boat motor sounded out on the bay. Dark was coming on, and we could see the shape of a speedboat making circles not far out from our landing. "AH-ROOH, AH-ROOH!" someone hollered. Then the boat turned toward Gull Inlet and we could hear it speeding toward Wistero Beach.

"Sam's got it right. They're real jerks," I said.

Louise giggled. "In their speedboat, maybe, but I bet they wouldn't be caught dead in that jungle at night."

"I'd just love to get 'em there to find out," I snickered, like I was all that brave myself.

Then Louise started strumming, and we sang some songs that made me homesick for Mirror Mountain. Soon my eyelids just wouldn't stay open. I stretched out on the cot in my clothes and didn't know a thing till morning broke.

# 11
# Lester's Room

Back on Mirror Mountain, Midnight woke me up just about every morning. Now it was pesky Louise. She was shaking a ring of keys over my head. "I found these in Uncle Jake's room yesterday," she said. "We need to see what's making noises in Lester's room."

I rubbed my eyes. "You know Uncle Jake don't want nobody going in there, Louise."

"He won't have to know. I'd hate for rats to chew up what's so valuable to him."

"Why? Don't nobody use none of it."

"Please, Johnny. I don't want to go in there all by myself."

It did me good to see a helpless look in Louise's eyes for a change. Also, I was more than a mite curious to see what Uncle Jake was so bent on locking away from us.

A few minutes later I picked up a piece of cold cheese toast from the kitchen and followed my sister down the hall. She tried keys till she found the right one.

There was a mighty squawk when we pushed open the door. Right off, we heard fast, rustling sounds like something living had been disturbed.

Dark green blinds shut the daylight from Lester's room. I felt around till I found a light switch. A dusty ceiling light came on. Just as quick, I saw a batlike critter pull its furry tail through the top slats of a window blind. It was too big to be a bat, but I knew what it was.

"Flying squirrels!" I yelled. I ran over and opened the blinds. A top corner pane was missing from the window. Pushing right up to it on the outside, the branch of a big cassina holly was still shaking. Sam had told me the tree's name. Its leaves were smooth and thick, with no sharp edges to nick you.

"The one flying out was the mama!" I was still excited.

We found her nest of five squiggly babies on top of an old wardrobe. It was easy to lift the nest from the wardrobe onto the bed. Flying squirrels aren't scared of people.

I reached in and picked up one of the babies. It made a squeaky little noise and crawled up on my shoulder.

"How cute!" Louise picked up another one. We sat awhile and let all the friendly little critters climb over us. They tickled our skin and made us chuckle.

We'd forgot about their mama till she dropped down smack in the middle of the bed. Before anyone could say "scat," she rolled one baby into a little ball, then caught up its loose belly with her teeth.

There was a skimpy curtain on the side of the window. In no time flat, she hauled her child up the curtain and through the broken pane. They disappeared in the leaves.

Shortly, mama squirrel glided right back in and picked up another baby, then another.

The last two babies were still snuggled against our necks. I think we were both hoping she would forget them. But that youngun-packing mama could count. She made two more trips. She climbed right up our shoulders and got the babies like it was something she did every day.

"Now we can close the window so they can't come back," Louise said. "Six flying squirrels could make a grand mess in here."

I took the nest out to the tree and set it high as I could in a tight place between branches. "You might not want to use it anymore," I said into the air, "but here it is, little mama." Not a single squirrel was showing, but I like to think critters understand when you do the best you can for them.

Louise covered a piece of heavy cardboard with

aluminum foil. She found some duct tape in Uncle Jake's room, and I closed up the open place. "Maybe it'll hold till we get a new pane and some putty," I said before I took a good look around the room.

The squirrels had knocked some of Lester's model ships from their shelves. It was a wonder that those in bottles were not broken. His bedspread had ships all over it, and there was a big banner on the wall that said U.S. NAVY.

What really grabbed my eye was Lester's ten-speed bike. It looked so lonesome. I went and sat on it. I had never owned a bike, but Ray Arthur, my cousin, did. I learned to ride it when I went to see him at Uncle Elbert's highway store.

"Get off that wheel and move stuff for me to mop and dust, Johnny." It was Louise, the cleaning maniac, coming back to bug me again. All morning I helped her clean up Lester's dirty room. I could have been fishing all that time, I thought. But I didn't say so out loud.

It was almost noon when Louise told me to put the vacuum cleaner away in the hall closet. When I came back, she was picking up cleaning rags.

I went over and sat on Lester's ten-speed again.

"You can stay there till I put these rags in the washer, Johnny. But when I'm done with that, we better lock up and put the keys back where I found 'em," she said as she left.

I looked around the room. It was a real boy's room

and I would have been so happy to have one just like it in our little house on Mirror Mountain.

When I heard footsteps, I figured it was Louise coming back down the hall. I thought, *hey, I been nice all morning, I'll move off this bike when I'm good and ready, no matter how loud she yells.*

But it wasn't Louise who brought me back to how things really were. It was Uncle Jake who stormed through the door. "WHAT YOU DOING IN HERE, BOY?" he shouted.

I whirled around. His eyes were round as marbles, glaring at me like an old cur gone mad.

Louise came hurry-scurry behind him. "Uncle Jake, I can explain," she begged. "We were…"

Uncle Jake would not take his wild eyes from my face. "Stop protecting him, Mollie," he yelled. "The boy has to learn to…" His neck bones stuck out and his face was red. He stood there all drawn up like a screen door with a spring so tight, it could not stretch a tidbit without whamming into you. I tried to get off the bike, but I couldn't seem to move.

Then something strange happened. Uncle Jake seemed to go limp like a dishrag. He plopped down on Lester's bed and put his face in those big, bony hands.

"Lester, boy," he whispered in a hoarse voice, "it was me that said you could join up. I told your ma she couldn't keep babyin' you. I told her the Navy'd make you into a real man." His shoulders were going up and

89

down and his breath came out in choppy puffs. "It was me, son—oh, please forgive me for sendin' you off to be killed." Then Uncle Jake started crying out loud.

Louise scooted over and threw her arms 'round him. "Oh, no, Uncle Jake. Don't you ever think that. Accidents happen. It wasn't 'cause of nothing you done." Her eyes got big and scared looking. "Now listen to me, Uncle Jake. Where's your nitroglycerin tablets?"

He fished a tiny bottle from his shirt pocket. Louise opened it and watched him put one under his tongue.

That was when I managed to get off the bike and out of there. In another minute, Uncle Jake might stop calling me Lester. Then he would remember I was the boy he didn't like anymore. In all my twelve years, I couldn't remember anyone actually hating me. It was more than I could handle. Like a rotten coward, I took off down the bay path to Sam's house.

The Simmonses' little home was new looking. It was painted light yellow, with flowers blooming in window boxes. I pushed open the back screen door and hurled myself into the kitchen.

"Uncle Jake hates my guts!" I blurted out, crying like a little youngun. What was worse, I didn't even care. I told them everything that went on in Lester's room.

Sae seemed surprised Uncle Jake had called me Lester and talked to Louise like she was Aunt Mollie.

"Jake seemed fine when I left him at the house," she went on. "All of his tests turned out good. The doctor said he just needs to get more exercise."

"Then let him exercise without me!" I bellowed. "I ain't going back to that house." I tried to stop sobbing, but my shoulders jerked like crazy. I didn't look at Sam. Seeing a Vandal Buster bawl must have been downright disappointing for him.

Then Sae walked over and put her arms 'round me. She patted me and said everything would be all right. It was just like Louise had done with Uncle Jake.

About that time, a light seemed to go on in my brain. Uncle Jake had been so strong and sure of himself before he lost his family. I had looked up to him like he was some kind of hero. Now it was plain that he was just lonely and scared and needed someone to hug him, somebody to tell him everything would turn out all right.

Soon the jerking stopped. In Sae's ma-like arms, I quieted down inside. I felt Preacher Abe's strong hand closing around mine. While all of us held hands, he prayed for God's perfect love to "drive out all fear." He prayed the hurting between me and Uncle Jake would heal.

Now I felt stronger. I hadn't studied it out yet, but I knew it had to do with how Sae and Preacher Abe had loved the hurt and fear out of me.

Preacher Abe and Sam took me home in the *Chariot* and went with me to see Uncle Jake. He and

Louise were sitting on the swing. Ma's old uncle looked so helpless. I knew just what I had to do.

I walked up to him and hugged his craggy old neck. "I'm sorry I upset you, Uncle Jake."

There wasn't all that much coming back to me, but he didn't pull away. Maybe, for then, that was enough for me to go on.

Louise excused herself to go in and warm up the last of the chicken bog. Sam and I left Preacher Abe and Uncle Jake talking and my friend helped me cut up celery and carrots for salad.

I fixed my eyes on what my hands were doing. Now that I was calmer, I felt ashamed before Sam. I didn't talk and he didn't try to make me till we finished the salad. Then I felt his arm on my shoulder like he just accidently dropped it there.

"Don't string your pride so tight, John E.," he almost whispered. "You oughta see the big shew I put on when I'm scared or hurt."

I couldn't help but grin. We slapped hands and went back to clowning around as usual.

Preacher Abe left for Wistero Beach, but Sam stayed to help us finish the chicken bog.

"Jeep phoned me this morning," he told us after Uncle Jake went to his room. "The Vandal Busters are going to meet at Deepwood House this afternoon."

# 12
# The Widow's Walk

Jeep met us just before we got to Deepwood House. "We'll sneak through the shrubbery on our side and come up the side steps," she said. "That's Meg's apartment below ours on the first floor, left. It's empty except when she comes to use it herself."

I filed along with the others after Jeep. She led us through shrubbery. Then we followed her up some steps to the second floor. When we got to the top of the stairs, she motioned us to be quiet. We could hear the soft clack-clack of Mr. Clark's word processor coming from that side of the upstairs hall. In the apartment on the other side, a TV set was on. Oprah Winfrey was interviewing some excited women. We could hear them raising and lowering their voices.

Jeep opened a door on the right and we went up a dark, narrow stairway that took us into a big attic crammed with old furniture. At the far end of the room, we climbed up a ladder and out of a trap door to the roof.

We were at the tip-top of the high old house on a flat-railed balcony. All around us were miles of green jungle. I squinted against the late afternoon sun to see cows in the big pasture behind the barn. Slag's pea-green pickup was parked in front of it. Down a bluff on the other side was Gull Inlet, marshes and the ocean. Sam pointed out Conch Island.

"Why do you call this a widow's walk?" I asked.

"It goes way back," Jeep said. "Most of the time, when a seafaring man built his home, he built a little balcony over the roof so his wife could stand on it and watch for his ship to come in."

"Sounds like it oughta be called a wife's walk," I said.

She shook her head, slowlike. "Sometimes the ship never came, Johnny. The husband would be lost at sea." She peeped down through the rails at the front drive. "Sherman's back."

We scrambled over for a look. A pinched-faced man got out of a red sports car and walked toward the house. Sherman wore a white polo shirt and long shorts.

" 'E looks like 'e got a whiff of that rotten fish," Sam said.

"Oh, Sam, he can't help how close his nose is to his

mouth," Louise said. She was right. But we laughed a little bit till Sam reminded us why we were there.

We settled down next to the chimney over Mr. Barnes's apartment. With the cover on the chimney, we could barely hear his TV going.

"This meeting of the Vandal Busters of Deepwood Bay will please come to order right now!" Sam's "right" sounded like "rate." You would have thought he had a pulpit in front of him. "Now, my fellow Vandal Busters, it has been confirmed that our prime suspect, namely the ill-famed Voodoo Boone, has departed this life forever and ever. Reliable sources have informed me that she most likely will not be returning to this island. Therefore, it appeahs we can no longer consider her to be under investigation."

"Mr. President, may I interrupt to say something?" Jeep had her hand up.

"With my permission, Miss Secretary." He motioned her to go on.

"Let's just review what we know about the real criminal."

I raised my hand and got Sam's go-ahead. "So far, it looks like he travels on foot."

"Right," agreed Louise. "This vandal knows his way around the plantation."

Jeep narrowed her eyes and folded her arms tight. "And it has to be somebody with something to gain by hauling smelly garbage through the jungle at night."

Sam scratched his head. "It does appeah to be so."

Then his old hate-Vick-and-Kevin snarl started to fester.

Jeep clicked her tongue. "Sam, get real. Why would rich guys with nice homes and fine boats go to all that trouble?"

Louise nodded. "Kevin said they didn't know where Bay Road was. They probably don't even know there is a church back in the woods."

Sam's eyes narrowed. "You girls sure are sweet on the dudes."

"Shhh! It's snooping time." Jeep stood up and leaned over the top of the chimney.

The television noise had stopped. We crowded around her as she unlatched and slid the top off the chimney.

"Come in, Sherman," we heard a man say in a deep voice.

"That's Mr. Barnes talking," Jeep whispered. Our heads kept bumping together as each of us tried to get an ear down to the opening.

"Hope you have good news," Mr. Barnes said.

"Not quite yet," said Sherman whose voice was high and tinny. "I've got someone working on persuading the blacks to sell the church property."

"Well, we can't wait much longer. Unless the deal shapes up soon, the company's going to close on another location for the marina."

"Jim, you're not going to find a better site than the mouth of the North River."

"I might get better cooperation from property owners on the next island, though." Mr. Barnes sounded like he was getting a mite upset. "We need easier land access to the marina. Something better than an old dirt road that meanders for miles through the jungle!"

"I expect Meg Duncan to sign for her part any day now. I sent her the papers. I advised her to sell some of the island property to cut down on taxes. She agreed on the phone it's the smart thing to do."

"Well, we can't wait much longer. The crews are in place to start construction on the new highway as soon as we get the property cleared. The marshes by the river need to be filled in, and we need that old church out of the way. I would think those blacks would jump at our generous offer."

"Don't worry, Jim," said Sherman. "There are ways to get these Gullah negroes to come around. You just have to know how to handle 'em."

"Well, I hope so. I'm leaving tomorrow. Here's the phone number where I can be reached." There was a short silence. "If I don't hear from you, I'll contact you in about two weeks for the final word."

"Trust me," Sherman said. "Now, if you'll excuse me, Jim, I have business with the caretaker. I just saw him come from the barn."

We heard footsteps, then the sound of a door opening and closing.

# 13
# Something Missing

I slid the cover back on the chimney for Jeep, then stole a worried look at Sam's face. Nobody seemed to know how to make him feel better over Sherman Attaway's insulting remark about his people, but my mouth never quits trying.

"Sam, I'm so sorry. But that smart-mouthed weasel just ain't worth losin' your cool over. I reckon he don't know any better."

Sam looked at us, one by one. Then he put his hands together and said, "John E. is right. I never cared for the dude. We got more important stuff to think about."

It was getting late. Sunsets on the island lasted longer than on the mountain. Puffy clouds went from pink to purple finally to blue-grey.

"Sherman's true colors certainly came shining through," Jeep remarked. "But I can't imagine Mr. Fancy-Pants himself doing the vandalizing."

"No way," Louise agreed. "But you can pretty well figure he's the one who called the sheriff about seeing four black younguns on the road Saturday night."

"We're on the right track," Sam said. "That hoity-toity snitch wouldn't stink up 'is lily white hands on rotten fish, much less carry it in a sack. And 'e wouldn't have the guts to go in that jungle at high noon, much less at night."

Jeep fixed Sam with a knowing grin. "Of course not. You heard him tell Mr. Barnes he's got somebody else working on it. He must be getting a lot in this deal, enough so he can easily afford to pay somebody else to do his dirty work."

"We need solid proof," said Louise. "So far, all we got's hearsay."

Sam snorted. "I don't understand what happened to Meg Duncan, agreeing to sell. She always acted like she loved this plantation."

"Maybe she's being tricked," said Jeep.

I thought about Deepwood Plantation with its green woods and marshes full of living things. I thought of how I might feel if developers came hacking away at Mirror Mountain. I had heard about it going on in other places. Some people don't care about keeping the mountains and islands the way God made them. They just care about making money.

"What would happen if a paved road got built through the jungle?" I asked.

Even when she frowned, I liked to look at Jeep's face. "I'm not real sure, Johnny, but my dad could tell us. Let's go ask him."

We followed her down to the apartment across the hall from Mr. Barnes's. There was a big room with a sofa and roomy chairs. Mr. Clark sat with books and papers around him and peered at us over his computer. His desk was a big oak table.

Jeep had eyes like her good-looking dad. As he sat there, I noticed he wasn't real tall, but was friendly like Jeep. "Have a seat, guys," he said, smiling. "I'll be with you soon as I save this chapter."

We watched him hit some keys and buttons. Then he swung his swivel chair away from the table to listen to us. We told him what we had heard on the widow's walk. Since he was a grown-up, I thought he might start up on us about eavesdropping, but his mind was working on the other stuff we told him.

He folded his hands and sighed. "So they plan to cut a highway through the plantation jungle to the mouth of the North River." He got up and looked through his window at the green woods. "If they do, many ancient oaks will be sacrificed. Precious marshland will be dredged and filled in."

Jeep's eyes were big and round and more purple-blue than ever. "Wouldn't that hurt the environment, Dad?"

"You'd better believe it would. The warming up of the earth is already taking place. Heat causes the ocean to expand. The more tidal wetlands get drained by developers, the sooner erosion occurs on our beaches. Life that depends on the marshes will cease. In short, the marshes will literally die."

"Does Meg know that?" Sam asked.

"I would think so. On the other hand, we've just learned something Meg probably doesn't know. And my guess is there's even more yet to be learned." He turned around and picked up his phone. "Jeep, why don't you get your friends something to drink in the kitchen." He sat down again. "I have some phoning to do just now."

We stayed in the kitchen long enough to finish our drinks. It was plain Mr. Clark wanted his privacy. Jeep led us down the front stairs into a big hall that ran from the front door to the back. The walls were lined with shelves of nothing but dolls.

Louise just went crazy over them. "Who do they belong to?" she asked Jeep.

"Mrs. Slatton. She makes them. See the bridal parties she has over there?"

Louise stood and looked at the sets of brides and grooms. There were bridesmaids and groomsmen, even flower girls and ring bearers that were all made from cloth.

The front screen door banged and Irene Slatton came tromping down the hall with her nose in the air like some feisty bird claiming its territory. She was about average size, I'd say, for a woman.

"Don't you children dare touch those dolls!" She squawked. "People won't buy dirty dolls at craft fairs."

"Y-you make all these dolls?" Louise asked. "They're real pretty."

"Thank you for saying so." Mrs. Slatton sniffed the

air. Then she smiled and showed a mouthful of square, straight teeth. Her long nose was shaped like a sliding board and she had a big mole on the end of it. The pink in her cheeks looked out of place.

Jeep introduced me and Louise, and Sam said "How you do, Mrs. Slatton." She nodded at him.

"Look, but don't touch," Irene went on. "If we could live in Charleston, I'd have my own shop. Out here in the woods, my talent's just hidden away." She sighed and headed for her apartment. "Got to check on my roast," she said over her shoulder. When she opened the door, the steamy smell of beef and onions came through. It made me hungry.

Finally, we got Louise all the way to the front porch. Sherman Attaway was in the driveway talking to Slag beside his car. Whatever Sherman was saying, you could tell it wasn't to Slag's liking. He shook his long, greasy hair and blinked his piglike eyes. Then Sherman grabbed him by the sleeve of his dirty T-shirt and held on to it. It was like he was trying to shake some sense into Slag, but there was no way a puny little man like Sherman could shake more than burly old Slag's shirtsleeve. The tussle ended as quickly as it had started.

Jeep walked with us past the men, and all the way to the road. I looked back and saw a curtain move in one of the windows of the Slatton apartment.

We had barely reached the road when Sherman's sporty red car pulled out of the drive with a mighty screech. He sped on down the road, leaving us in a cloud of dust.

I coughed. "Wonder what that was all about?"

"Looks like Sherman was puttin' pressure on 'is hit man," Sam said.

Jeep agreed. "Slag takes all of his orders from Sherman, all right."

"While Irene makes dolls." Louise was smiling like she had some fine secret.

"Come on, Louise," I said. "You put me in mind of Midnight snitchin' a chunk off one of my fatback biscuits. Might as well tell us."

"All right. There's a groom doll missing from one of the wedding party sets in the hall."

"So?" Sam waved his long fingers in the air.

"I'm surprised nobody but me noticed. The voodoo doll at the church was dressed exactly like the groom dolls. It had to be stolen from Irene's collection."

"You mean…" I looked at Sam. His mouth was open like what hit me had just landed on him, too.

Jeep walked with us as far as the mailboxes by the big oak, then turned to jog back to Deepwood House.

Louise was still acting biggety about noticing that old doll was missing. "Slag must have stolen that groom doll to leave on the church steps with sticks in it," she said. "Bet if Irene finds out, she'll be plenty mad at him."

Something else came to me, though. "Unless she blames us for taking it," I said. "You know how she

103

warned us not to touch 'em."

Sam scratched his head. "You're right, John E. If Slag's the vandal, 'e might find it. Then 'e'd say, 'Irene, baby, let's take a walk.' Then 'e'd lead her down the church lane and fix it so she'd just find the doll."

I took it from there. "He'd get away with sayin' one of us must have stolen it today. Irene might even call the sheriff."

Sam whirled around. "John E., we got to go back and get rid of that doll right now!"

Louise said no, we had chores to do, and Irene didn't strike her as one to walk anywhere when she didn't have to.

The next morning when Sam and I went to check on the church, we went to where the doll was hidden. We got on our knees and flung straw all over the place like two hungry thrashers scratching for worms.

Finally I sat back on my heels. I wondered if my face looked as flabbergasted as Sam's. The doll was just plain gone.

# 14
# Signs of
# Change

"It appeahs Mister Sherman Attaway's not handling us Gullahs too superbly." Sam's grin was full of devilment that morning as we walked back to Deepwood Bay after checking on the church.

It was going on two weeks since we had overheard Sherman Attaway's promise to Mr. Barnes. We were surprised that the vandal had not struck during that time. We had staked it out on Friday and Saturday nights of last week, but not one vandal had shown up.

I gave a half-grin and shrugged. "I purely looked for ole Slag to come around last weekend."

"Maybe we scared the pants off 'im. You know, when 'e brought the sack of fish."

"We scared him all right, but I think he's just gonna

lay low a spell," I said. "You recollect Mr. Barnes giving Sherman till the end of this week to get his dirty work done?"

"I do. We'd best watch Slag real close from now on."

Earlier we had left Uncle Jake walking on the bay shore like the doctor told him, which was one sign that he was getting better. He looked so much more like himself in his old fishing cap and T-shirt, with his scrawny knees hanging out below his Bermuda shorts.

Just last Sunday, the Vandal Busters had gone with Uncle Jake to his church. The people didn't clap or raise their hands to praise God, but they were real friendly. I was glad I didn't forget my Bible. The preacher used his a lot.

Like I said, Uncle Jake was coming around. I wouldn't be so rash as to say it happened right off. He still looked out at nothing I could see sometimes, but after that day he kinda fell apart in Lester's room, he let me do more for him.

One morning I had fetched his socks and shoes. When I brought them to him on the porch, I noticed his long toenails. They had clean dug holes in the toes of his socks. I hunted up some clippers and trimmed them. Then I filled a basin with warm salt water for him to soak his feet.

Seeing how Uncle Jake liked that, I got Louise's manicure set and trimmed and filed his fingernails, too. His nails were tough and dry—dry like my mouth felt just then. I got in Louise's way long enough to fix two glasses of orange juice. Out on the bay, gulls wheeled through the air. Clapper rails, little marsh birds with real long toes, called "cac-cac-cac" from the tall grass they were hiding in. Uncle Jake and I sat back and drank our orange juice in pure contentment.

"It's about time me and you went fishing," I said.

Uncle Jake nodded. "We going soon's I get some things done. Can't nobody else tend to 'em. Then we'll drown some crickets, Johnny." Yep, old Uncle Jake was coming back and I was pleased as punch.

While Sam and I took our own sweet time going home, a car passed us. When we got back to Deepwood Bay Uncle Jake was talking to the people who were in it.

A woman and two younguns were there with scooped-out milk cartons. I knew right off what that meant. Mr. McFaddin had pretty much said he would send more shell hunters. I just didn't expect it to be so soon.

I thought about the $15 that was still under my mattress. Now Uncle Jake would find out from someone else how I had disobeyed him. *Woe is me,* I thought as he crooked his old finger at me.

Uncle Jake did not crack the tiniest kind of smile. He just looked at me real hard and said, "I hear you're a good boat pilot, Johnny."

One teensy hole in the sand was what I looked for. I would have been ever so thankful to slide into it like a fiddler crab at low tide.

"Uncle J-Jake," I said weakly, "I was aimin' to tell you and g-give you…"

"Never mind," he said. His eyes were still set tight, like they might cut clean through me. "These people want to go to Conch Island and I'm too busy to take them myself. The tide's right, so how 'bout gettin' with it, sailor!"

Then he cut his eye at me. I had seen that half-teasing, proud kind of mischief in Ma's eyes lots of times. I knew Uncle Jake was fighting the corners of his mouth to keep a big smile from spreading.

Sam looked as pleased as I felt, but didn't offer to go along. It was like he knew I wanted to grab hold and run the tour by myself. Anyhow, Uncle Jake had already told Sam he wanted to talk to him about painting some new tour signs.

Before I aimed the boat towards Conch Island, I turned and waved back at them.

Later, when I got back and sent the happy family on their way, I put up the gear. Then I marched straight to my cot and pulled the $15 from under the mattress.

Sam had gone home. At the other end of the porch, Uncle Jake was touching up fishing lures with some of Louise's red nail polish.

I walked down to him and held out the money from both tours. "This money's yours," I told him. "I know I ought to've told you sooner that I took some people to the island." Then I heard myself telling him why I didn't. "I never planned to use the money myself." If I had to get myself busted, I might as well lay it all out in the open.

Boy, was I ever glad I did. It wasn't just that Uncle Jake trusted me with his boat. He went on to say he never believed for a minute that I had taken his money for keeps. He took the money and gave me back half. "Long as you're on this island, we're partners, Johnny."

I felt like a hot-air balloon floating over the bay, and that was before I saw Lester's shiny ten-speed leaning against the wall in the sunlight.

That night I went to my new room and wrote to Ma and Pa.

I still miss you and Aunt Lou. I was homesick, but not anymore. Uncle Jake is getting pert as a cricket. He gave me Lester's room. I told Louise she could have it, but she said she likes the dinning room better. O yes I also have a bike to ride. Maybe we will come home soon. I love you. Johnny Elbert.

The next day Uncle Jake was in the kitchen finishing up a bowl of oatmeal when first Sam, then Jeep showed up. Mr. Clark had gone to Charleston for the day. Louise had asked Sam to stay for dinner, too.

Sam wore a big old shirt that had paint all over it. He set his oil paints on the steps and stood in front of Uncle Jake. Folding his hands, he bowed almost to his ankles. Then he came up grinning. "Super Sam serves

superbly!" He announced. "I'm here to redo the signs."
He finished with a little strut that made us laugh.

Uncle Jake's old tour signs were piled up in the car
shed. I helped Sam put on the first coat of white paint
to cover the faded-out words.

"Man, I got some good ideas for signs that'll stop
traffic." Sam looked happy as a cat with a belly full of
vittles.

We worked till noon, and knocked off to eat dinner.

That afternoon we were putting on the second coat
when Vick and Kevin pulled in at the landing in the
speedboat. They hung around and watched us till the
girls came out. It was downright disgusting how Kevin
shined right up to Jeep.

"I thought you might show us Deepwood House,"
he said to her. "That is, you and Louise." He looked at
me standing there with paint all over me. "I see that
you guys can't leave your project just now," he said.

Louise and Jeep looked at me and giggled.

I acted like I didn't notice. It was purely sickening
how the girls went walking off with those two jerks,
hanging on to every stupid thing they said.

After we couldn't see them anymore, Sam and I
cleaned the brushes. He told me how he planned to
decorate the signs. But first, he had to wait for the
second coat of white paint to dry. It seemed like a
good time for a quick bike ride down Bay Road.

Sam never told me he had a bike till Uncle Jake let
me use Lester's. "Biking's no fun when you got a

buddy without one," he explained to me. It's not every day you get a buddy like Sam.

We whizzed past Deepwood House. Vick was taking a picture of Kevin who had an arm around each girl's shoulder. None of them seemed to know or care what fools they were making of themselves.

"Watch out, John E!" Sam yelled. I just missed hitting a rabbit that ran in front of me.

"Girls—nothing but trouble," Sam warned.

I upped my chin. "Don't bother me none." Maybe if I said it enough, I might get my feelings where my mouth was.

Everything looked in place at the church, so we headed back to Deepwood Bay.

It seemed like hours before the others got back to Uncle Jake's landing. Jeep was smiling, showing her dimples. The end of a little book was sticking out of Kevin's shirt pocket. So she had gone and given him her shell book. So what? I was nothing to her and she sure as shooting wasn't anything to me. Oh, shucks!

Sam wasn't long painting decorative borders on the signs. He finished three of them saying SHELL TOURS—$3 PER PERSON. CALL JAKE SHOPE AT 869-9800 BETWEEN 4:30 P.M. and 5:00 P.M. ONLY.

All of us went up where Uncle Jake was sitting on the porch cleaning up his telephone. "Reckon I'll be needing this," he said. "I thought you younguns might want to keep in touch with each other, too."

Vick and Kevin left to go home. They didn't act like

fools taking off this time. Maybe they were getting nicer. No matter. I felt better when they were out of sight.

Sam went on home, too. It would soon be dark and the two of us aimed to stake out the church that night.

I went down to the boat house, plopped on a bench and let the breeze curl 'round my ears.

I sure was surprised to look up and see Jeep. She sat down next to me. Her eyes were just shining, and I had to bite my lip to keep from asking why she was so all-fired happy. Then she commenced to tell me.

"For the very first time in my entire life, I led someone to the Lord today," she said. "I never thought I could."

I didn't know what to say. "I don't spect nobody gets led where he don't want to be took."

"That's what Preacher Abe told me, Johnny. But this afternoon Kevin prayed the prayer with me and accepted Christ into his heart. God used me—Jeep Clark!"

"Well, glory be!" I didn't mean to sound sarcastic. It just came out that way.

"Please don't make fun of me," she went on. "Vick and Kevin are really good guys. Their parents just don't have much time for them. They need to know they're loved, that God loves them. Won't it be great if Kevin tells Vick and Vick gets saved and both win their parents and…"

"Slow down, Jeep. That's up to the Lord. I'd say

you done your part. And you went and gave Kevin your shell book. I saw it sticking out of his pocket. I reckon you like him a whole lot." That just had to slip out of my mouth.

Her purplish blue eyes got big and wide, and she slowly shook her head. "Oh, Johnny. You thought that was my shell book? It was a little New Testament I gave him."

I looked down at my sneakers as they stirred up the sand.

Jeep touched my arm. Her soft, warm hand felt light as a butterfly. I could feel myself blushing clean up to my puny brain.

"Now hear this, Johnny Elbert Finlay," she said. "I like Kevin in a friendly way. You're my friend, too, but I really like you a lot. I admire you and Louise for being so good to Mr. Jake. Someday when I'm grown up, I hope I'll marry some guy like you. . . . Oh my!" She clamped her hand over her mouth quicklike, and that did tickle me good. Soon both of us just reared back and laughed. After that, I walked her almost all the way home. Seeing her so happy made me hope the Lord would see fit to use me that way one day.

Sam and I didn't stake out the church that night, after all. Jeep said Slag and Irene had gone to a craft show at Myrtle Beach, which was almost to North Carolina. They would be real late getting home. Too late for lazy old Slag to do any vandalizing.

# 15
# Hot on the Vandal Trail

The next day, Sam and Jeep were both on their own, so we asked them to spend the day with us. Mr. Clark had gone to Charleston on business again, and Sam's parents left early for an all-day meeting on Saint Helena Island.

"Some people there are working on a Gullah Bible," Sam told us. "Papa says the Gullah people held on to how they talked and did things in Africa. It was mostly because they didn't get sold all over the south like other slaves. They stayed on the islands. 'E says my children's children gonna be glad for a Bible that reads just like their ancestors talked."

Sam looked real proud about all that. Louise said she was going to get Aunt Lou to talk about the Finlays on Mirror Mountain. She said she was going to write it down to pass on just like Sam's people were doing.

Uncle Jake liked Sam's signs with their borders of seashells, palmettos, and egrets. We put one on the big oak near the mailboxes, and Sam set one aside to go in front of the Wistero Beach Post Office. After that we fished off the log till Louise and Jeep called us to dinner.

Jeep served me the biggest piece of the apple pie, and I caught Uncle Jake winking at Sam. I knew they were warming up to lay some teasing on me later, but I didn't care.

Uncle Jake wanted the largest sign to go on a big sycamore at the forks on Bay Road. He offered to drive us there late that afternoon, but we wanted to take our bikes. We could tie the sign on one of them with ropes.

It was late afternoon before the four Vandal Busters rode down Bay Road. Jeep and Louise were riding double on Jeep's ten-speed. The sign and tools rode with Sam and me.

"We'll check by the church coming back," Sam decided. "We can hide the rope for tonight's stakeout. We might need it."

"We better hide it better'n we did that old voodoo doll," I said.

"Did I hear you say voodoo doll?" Jeep cut in. "I got rid of that for good."

"Say what?" Sam craned his long neck her way.

"I meant to tell you. I went back the same day Louise noticed it missing from Irene's collection."

Then she went on to say she thought about returning it to Irene, but didn't. "The doll was used to

115

put an evil curse on Preacher Abe. It didn't work, of course, but the Bible tells us to destroy any object used for occult purposes. So I built a fire and burned it."

"Well, you did right, Yankee girl," said Sam. "It's one thing we don't need to worry about."

We had set the bikes at low speed because of the stuff we had to carry to put up the sign.

"Don't want no extras falling off," Sam said.

"Wouldn't hurt none to drop Louise," I joked.

"Go eat grass," Louise cut back at me, and everybody cackled.

After we passed Deepwood House and the church lane, we rode about two miles further to the forks. It didn't take us long to nail the new sign on the big sycamore tree. Then we started the long, slow ride back to Deepwood Bay.

There was a sharp bend in the road just before the church lane. You couldn't see around the curve till you were right there. When I think back, I still can't believe what happened next.

We rounded the bend just in time to see the tail end of Slag's pea-green pickup pull into the church lane, out of sight.

"Slag's going to the church right now," Jeep said real fast.

We speeded up the bikes.

"Just pray he didn't see us," Louise said.

"'E didn't," Sam called back. "But 'e soon will."

By now, we were at the church lane. With all the thick, moss-hung trees, and the lane curving the way it did, we couldn't see the church from where we were.

We hid our bikes in the bushes. "Got to cut through the jungle and sneak up on 'im," said Sam. He and I flung the two ropes over our shoulders. Then Sam motioned us to follow him.

"Wait," Louise said. "Somebody has to call the sheriff."

That made sense, and I knew who could handle that job. "So take my bike and do it," I said.

"We'll use our phone at Deepwood House," Jeep said in a hurry.

The girls took off faster than you could sneeze. I figured they didn't mind missing the walk through the jungle. I didn't much care to push through briars and snaky bogs, either.

Sam and I stayed close to the lane, though. As long as we had to watch for snakes and such, there wasn't time to think of what might happen later. It was when we stopped that I got trembling scared.

One thing was dead sure. No slow-moving sheriff was going to make it to the church right off. With Sam's parents and Mr. Clark gone, there was just Uncle Jake. Louise probably wouldn't feel he was well enough to be upset, which meant that for now, it was just me and Sam up against whomever. It was plain as my hand. We'd have to tackle that hefty bully of a

117

man all by ourselves.

Most likely, we had bitten off more than we could chew. Was this how soldiers felt just before they faced the enemy? In all my life, I had never wanted to turn tail and run like I did right then. But instead, I just took a couple deep breaths and prayed.

# 16
# Discovering Who Done It

Sam and I hunkered down behind some myrtles. The pea-green truck was near the back of the church. There, in plain daylight, stood the vandal in his stupid disguise. Slag's head was covered with the hood of a loose, floppy, dark coat, and he wore work gloves. A woman's stocking was pulled tight over his face. He didn't look big and heavy like I remembered, though.

"With all that garb on, Slag ain't up to no good," Sam whispered. "Why we waitin', John E.?"

"For him to do something criminal," I said. "We gotta catch him in the act." I wasn't about to let on to Sam how scared I was.

We watched Slag creep to the front of the church and look all around. We didn't dare to even breathe.

After a long minute, the vandal went to the tail of the pickup. He reached in and pulled two bags chock full of garbage from the truck bed. He swung one in each hand till he got up to the church. He turned both upside down. A lot of wadded-up newspaper tumbled out.

"That's proof!" Sam whispered. "Now, John E.?"

Somehow, I just knew it wasn't time. "Not yet."

We crept closer and closer, keeping out of sight. I wondered how little David ever got up the nerve to go out and slay that big, old Goliath. Except, of course, we weren't out to kill Slag. We just aimed to make sure he let Deepwood Bible Church be.

Slag, the hooded vandal, came back and reached in the back of the truck again to drag something toward him. When he got it to where we could see what it was, I sucked my breath in real fast. It was a big square can labeled KEROSENE.

He screwed the top off the can. Sam nudged me, but I still shook my head. One wrong move and we could blow the whole thing. My common sense told me we needed to wait till he started to light a fire. Then we would have to move real fast. We couldn't let him burn Deepwood Church. Up to now, Slag had just vandalized the church, which was bad enough. But this move of his was really wicked. This looked like outright arson.

"We need help. Send anybody, Lord," I prayed.

The would-be arsonist was sliding the heavy can out. That was plumb stupid. Why wouldn't a man as strong as Slag just pick it up?

All of a sudden, the can butted against something in the truck bed. Kerosene splashed out over Slag's floppy coat. He backed off. Still wearing gloves, he used both hands to lift the can. He set it down with a mighty grunt. From under the coat, he brought out a cigarette lighter. Holding it in one hand, he used the other one to drag the full can toward the pile of wadded newspaper. My heart skipped a beat.

"NOW!" I yelled, and we jumped out of the bushes.

The vandal whipped around like a bullet and stumbled over his long coat. The can tilted over and more pale yellow liquid ran out on the ground toward the pile of paper. At the same time, Slag flicked on the lighter he was still holding, then dropped it on the paper pile. The floppy coat blazed up all of a sudden like it might be the fourth of July.

"EEEEEEEEH!" The vandal's blood-curdling scream hurt my ears. For a man, it sure was high-pitched. Slag flopped around like a chicken with its head freshly wrung.

It pays to listen to and remember school safety rules. Sam and I both hollered, "DROP DOWN AND ROLL." When our advice sunk in, our vandal rolled and rolled in a bed of clover. Soon as we could, we grabbed the numbskull and yanked off his scorched coat. I held him down while Sam broke a branch from a myrtle bush. He swept the burning papers away from the kerosene, then beat the fire out of them.

I was sorely tempted to pound the vandal in the dirt,

but I didn't. I figured I had better leave well enough alone. I was amazed I was able to even pin down a grown man in the first place.

Sam came over and tugged at the stocking till he got it off the criminal's head.

"MY COW!" bellowed my friend. The whites of Sam's eyes got rounder and bigger. When I saw why, I almost let my charge wiggle loose.

It wasn't Slag's bald head he'd uncovered. A tangled mess of brassy blonde hair tumbled from the stocking.

What Irene Slatton said next, I could not rightly repeat. But she said it through those big, square teeth of hers, except when she was trying to bite me and twist herself away.

"Mrs. Slatton," Sam cried out, "you ought to be mortally ashamed of yourself!"

I was tying up her hands with the rope when we heard sirens coming. Right after the sheriff and his deputy got there, Tom Clark drove up with the girls in the backseat. A pretty woman sat beside Jeep's dad.

"It's Megan Duncan!" Sam exclaimed.

"They got to Deepwood House just as we were leaving to come back here," Jeep said.

The sheriff was reading Irene her rights when Slag came huffing and puffing from the jungle. When he saw his wife, his red face was some kind of mad. "I told you I wouldn't go so far's to burn no church!" he yelled.

Irene sucked in her breath and stuck out her bottom lip far enough for a june bug to ride on it.

"You fool," she snapped at Slag. "If you'd gone on and done it last night like Mr. Attaway said, we'd be rich and free." Well, she said something like that, with some cuss words worked in.

I heard a loud racket coming up the lane, and soon Uncle Jake showed up in his old Chevy. I found out later that Louise had called him after Jeep called the sheriff.

All the getting mad wasn't over with yet. Sherman's sniffy nose must have smelt trouble. He had followed Uncle Jake down the lane, but slammed on his brakes when he saw the sheriff's car. He started backing up real fast, but missed a curve and slammed into a tough old oak. The back end of that spiffy set of wheels was bent clean out of shape.

Slag went tearing down there and pulled Sherman out of the car. He shook that dinky little guy up, down, and around like he might be a football Slag was going to throw across the yard.

"You ain't gettin' off so easy," Slag yelled at the lawyer. "You never paid me a cent for all I done on this job. We gonna talk plenty, my wife and me."

Sherman's face was pinched and pale. He had hit his upper lip on the steering wheel, and it was bleeding. He kept trying to pull away, but Slag wouldn't let go.

The sheriff's big, strong deputy stepped in and led Slag to where Irene leaned against the sheriff's car. She was wearing handcuffs.

Sherman went into a tizzy. "I'm charging that man with attempted assault!" he squealed.

"Simmer down, Sherman Attaway," Meg cut in. "You're fired. I've got enough on you to press charges of my own!" The look on Meg's face told me she was telling it like it was. She told Slag and Irene she wouldn't be needing them anymore, either.

Sherman pranced back and forth with his hands in the air. "My poor car!" he wailed.

"For now, you just get in it and leave this plantation," ordered Meg. "I'll see you in court."

Somehow, Sherman managed to get his banged-up car on the road. The sheriff's car, with Irene in the back, followed. Slag came next in his pea-green pickup.

The four Vandal Busters were lined up beside Uncle Jake's old Chevy. Meg turned to us and said, "You are four terrific young people. I really admire you for what you've done. You cared about this church. You cared about saving the environment on this island." She looked at Jeep's dad. "When you called me, Tom, I realized Sherman had sent me fake plots of what he advised me to sell. Obviously, Sherman planned to attach the page with my signature to another one. That would be the set he would use to close the sale. He must have been planning to pocket the money and run."

"I knew you loved this plantation," Sam told her.

"I do. I would never agree to have Deepwood chopped up the way Sherman intended. That's why I've already signed papers for the greater part of the plantation to be preserved as a wildlife refuge."

Uncle Jake was standing between Louise and me like Ma and Pa would if they had been there.

"What'll happen to Slag and Irene?" Louise asked.

"Well, Irene's attempted arson is more serious than Slag's vandalism," Tom Clark said.

"I've had an auditor investigating the cattle sales," Meg said. "He found that Sherman and Slag have been selling beef cattle they wrote off as being lost or drowned in the bogs. This attempt to execute crooked land sales was just going to be the icing on their cake. Rest assured that Sherman will not go scot-free."

Sam clapped his hands together over his head. "Boy, oh boy, will Papa be surprised what 'e and Sae missed today," he said. "I can hardly wait to tell them Deepwood Church is safe again."

Jeep turned to Sam. "Looks like Vick and Kevin were innocent, doesn't it?"

Sam looked hacked. "Yeah, uh-huh. I reckon I got to take back all the bad mouthin' I did."

"And apologize to them for even thinking they did it."

"Jeepers, Jeep. They never knew. I, I don't owe 'em. . . ." He looked from Jeep to Louise, then to me. All of us just smiled nicely and nodded.

"Oh, all right. I'll tell 'em, but they better not laugh." Super Sam's chin went up. He balled up his fists and danced around, punching the air. "If they do, they gonna get this and this and this." Of course everybody laughed at the clown.

# 17
# From Wistero Island to Mirror Mountain

We stayed at Deepwood Bay till mid-July. By that time, Uncle Jake was trying to cram every day full of good old healthy living.

We got in some real good fishing. Sam was along most of the time, but I was always the one running the boat.

One day when it was just me and Uncle Jake, he said, "Johnny Elbert, you do put me in mind of Lester. That youngun could handle a boat when he was knee high to a duck. He wasn't short like you, but smart." He rubbed some wetness from the edge of his eye. It was okay with me. Sae told us it was good for him to shed a few tears.

"I reckon I'll always be squatty like Pa," I said.

"But tough. If Lester'd been here, he'd been staking out that church same as the rest of you. Johnny, you're something else again!"

We were having so much fun, I felt a little bit sad to leave. But Uncle Jake was cooking his own healthy food. He had a contraption to check his blood pressure, and he measured out his medicines once a week. Louise got him three 7-day pill boxes; morning yellow, midday white, and evening blue. He could get along just fine without us now.

Uncle Jake said maybe he could ship the bike to Cougarville. I told him not to do that. I told him, "Just keep it in Lester's room for me to ride when I come back to see you." Pa had promised to let me use his old dirt bike, now that he had Old Blue to drive.

Sam painted big VANDAL BUSTER T-shirts for all of us, and Jeep had him paint me a baseball cap to match my shirt. I wore it the day Uncle Jake took us in his boat to the bus station.

Jeep's big shirt matched her eyes. "Dad's finished the book and we're going home, too," she told me. "But I'll write to you, and you just better write me back."

I promised I would. Right then, I vowed to improve my writing faster than that girl from Connecticut talked. As for reading, I was already halfway through Exodus in my Living Bible.

"All aboard that's coming aboard!" Uncle Jake called. I took one last look at the egrets swooping down for vittles in the green marshes. My eyes got watery as chicken soup.

"Now don't you younguns go gettin' ch-choked up,"

127

Uncle Jake said. His Adam's apple twitched as he swallowed. "You gonna be back here together next summer. That's a promise!"

Everybody got in the boat, and in no time we were headed for Wistero Beach. Before the day was over, Pa and Ma would be meeting our bus at the foot of Mirror Mountain. It was good to be going home.